THE MOUNTAIN GHOST 4

The

Ghost   Twins

by

Vernon Gillen

Copyright © January 5, 2017 Vernon Gillen

All rights reserved. No part of this book may be reproduced or transmitted in any form or by any means, electronic or mechanical, including photocopying, recording, or by an information storage and retrieval system, without permission from the author or publisher.

All of Vernon's book are available at Amazon.com

ISBN - #

978- 1984197535

Contents

Chapter		Page
1.	The Ghost Warriors	6
2.	The Guns	20
3.	Lieutenant Bakers	34
4.	The Depot	48
5.	The Warehouse	62
6.	The River	76
7.	Myers	90
8.	Jenifer's Quest	103
9.	The Search	115
10.	Ghost Warriors	127
11.	Death Ghost	140
12.	My Home	153
13.	The Mexican Connection	167

Chapter 1

The Ghost Warriors

Over the past seventeen years Russ and June's twin daughters, Jenifer and Ann grew to be quite the warriors. From age three their father had been teaching them how to survive and fight; how to be the best Mountain Ghosts ever. However; they preferred to call themselves the Ghost Twins. They even toyed with the name, Twin Ghosts but, that did not sound as good.

The Chinese brought in almost half a million more Chinese and North Korean soldiers through California and raised their control in Arizona, Nevada, New Mexico and western Texas. However; they lost everything east of the Mississippi. Most of the North Korean soldiers headed to the Mississippi River never made it there making that area weak.

With over three million Chinese and North Korean soldiers in the southern part of the United States it looked like the entire fifty states would never be reunited again. But, Chinese Command in Austin, Texas did not know about the Ghost Twins.

Russ was barely able to walk due to being shot in the back leaving a bullet against his spin. Although the bullet was removed seventeen years earlier his spinal column would never be the same. Russ may not have been able to go back into battle but he was able to train his two daughters. Soon they would head south as the new Mountain Ghosts; although they would go by the name of Ghost Twins.

Lieutenant Haung was thought to be dead but instead he came back with a raise in rank to Lieutenant Colonel. He was also put in charge of the Centerville area; a position usually reserved for someone holding three ranks above him. He was given the rank and position because Chinese Command was impressed with his chasing the Mountain Ghost north into Free America. He was harder on the American people in that area than anyone else had been.

Lt. Colonel Haung did keep two things. He continued the newspaper which was full of lies and propaganda. He also kept the weekend trade days on the courthouse lawn but it had grown so much that it covered many square blocks of downtown Centerville. He used the trade weekends to scout the faces hoping to find wanted civilians.

Ever since Jenifer and Ann were three years old they had been training to take over as the new Mountain Ghosts. However; June did not like this. She saw them as pretty little ladies but Russ saw them as pretty little; vicious killers. Many of the young men in the Dallas area wanted to date the sisters but they were afraid of Russ. To be honest, Russ liked that. He did not want any hormone raging young man even being around his daughters.

There was one young man that Russ allowed close to his girls. His name was Brandon, the son of Dan and Bel-le. Brandon was named after Russ' brother who was killed by North Korean soldiers many years earlier. He was a tall young man and just as much of a fighter as Jenifer and Ann. When Russ started training his girls he also started training Brandon. The three spent the next fourteen years training together with their fathers at their sides.

The three of them worked so well with each other that sometimes they knew what the other was thinking about. When it came to Jenifer and Ann they really did know what the other one was thinking. Being exact twins, they had a connection between the two of them unmatched to anyone else.

One day the twins talked to their father about leaving Dallas and doing what they were trained all of their life to do. Although Russ understood how they felt a father never did like his little girls going out among danger. After a few days of arguing the twins told their father that they were leaving the next morning.

"Your training isn't finished." Russ argued.

"I don't want my little girls down there." June also argued.

"Oh my god ... Mom." Jenifer smirked.

"We're leaving tomorrow morning and that's that." Ann insisted.

"Is Brandon going too?" Russ asked.

"Yes Dad." Jenifer said.

"Does his father know?" Russ ask.

"Yes Dad." Jenifer said again.

The arguing continued until Dan and Brandon walked up. Dan was proud of what his son was about to do. "I guess your daughters told you the good news." Dan said to Russ and June.

"The girls ... little girls ... were just telling us." Russ said.

Dan was quiet for a moment and then said; They are no longer your little girls."

"They are if I say they are." Russ yelled at Dan.

"You have been training them to take over as the Mountain Ghosts but when were you planning to let them go?" Dan asked.

"But they're only seventeen years old." Russ still argued but lowered his tone of voice.

"And what age were you with you started fighting these Chinese and North Korean soldiers?"

"I don't remember." Russ snapped back.

"And you're a liar too Russ." Dan said with a firm voice. "You were about sixteen weren't you? Your daughters are almost eighteen years old; about two years older than the age when you started." Russ was quiet knowing that he had no defense. Dan continued saying; "You have trained them to do this. Now allow them to do it."

Russ stepped away as June fallowed. They held each other for a while and then turned to face the girls. Russ put a hand on each of the girls left shoulders and asked; "You will try to make me proud won't you?"

"Of course." Jenifer and Ann agreed. "Of course we will.

That night Brandon, Jenifer, and Ann packed their backpacks and got their rifles ready. Jenifer was born before

Ann so she got her father's 270 rifle. Ann carried a 308 caliber M-14 rifle with a 6x16 scope. The M-14 rifle was a bit heavier than the 270 rifle but Ann was stronger than her sister anyway. Brandon carried an AK-47. Wu lost his sniper rifle long ago in battle and had only the AK to pass on to his son.

The next morning everyone got together and met before the three left. Dan would drive them down to just south of Groesbeck to drop them off. From there they would be on their own. Russ and Dan did not know that all of the old Ghost Warriors were killed so they made sure the three knew where to find their old friends.

As Dan drove off with the three June and Bel-le started crying. When Russ was alone he cried as well but no one knew it. It was a man's thing.

Dan drove all night until he reached the home of Jack and Mary. The home had been burned down long ago. With daylight coming soon Dan parked the truck behind the barn which did not look much better than the home. As the sun came up they found the scattered bones of Jack and Mary in the back yard. They stayed in the trees until it was almost dark.

After it got dark Dan drove the three to Tom's home. They already knew that it had been hit by two bombs and a crashing Chinese MIG fighter jet but the many years had not been friendly to what was left over. As they looked in the fields they found the scattered bones of the many that had died fighting the North Koreans. Their father had told the story many times.

"Evidentially Dad didn't know about Jack and Mary's home but he told us about this." Ann said. "But I just did not picture this many of them dead."

What do you want to do now?" Dan asked the three.

"Sooner or later we have to strike out on our own; maybe make our own friends." Brandon said.

The girls agreed so Dan planned on leaving them there at Tom's place. "This is quite lonely out here now that everyone is gone but …" Dan said as he pointed a the trailer that used to belong to their parents. "… that's where your parents lived."

"Leave us Dad." Brandon said. "This is not easy but you need to leave us here so we can do our job."

Dan knew that he had to leave them sooner or later. "Okay then. I'll tell your parents where I left you." After that Dan got in the truck and drove off.

Finally the three were on their own. This is want they wanted but there was still a level of fear as well. They had no friends and no one that they could trust. They spent the rest of the day and that night there. Then they left out for Marquez the next morning but stuck to the trees so a black drone would not see them.

When Dan got back to Dallas he told Russ, June, and Belle where he dropped the three at. He also told them about Jack and Mary. The news hit Russ hard. Everyone he left there was dead and he blamed himself for leaving.

"Russ." Wu said. "When we put you in the back of that truck you were out of it. It was not like you had a choice. What happened would have happened anyway."

Russ looked down and agreed but the pain of knowing that he lost all of his friends was hard. Wu was right but it still hurt.

Only because Brandon was born a few hours first, the three had decided that he would be in charge long ago. Not having a leader to make final decisions is a big mistake. Sometimes there is no time to discuss something and one person must make the decision.

The one thing that the three never discussed was what to call themselves. Ghost Twins sounded good for just the two girls but he was part of the group as well. They still wanted to use the word ghost in their name so they would be associated with the original Mountain Ghost.

Finally Brandon suggested Ghost Warriors. It worked before. The only difference was that the Mountain Ghost was not leading it. After talking it over they all agreed. They would call themselves the Ghost Warriors.

It took a few days but they finally reached the trees just east of Marquez. After leaving their weapons they walked into town and talked to some the local people. It did not take long to make a couple of friends.

Butch and Eve lived across the railroad tracks in a shack he built long ago. They lived together only because there were no ministers around to marry them. When Brandon asked why they were not married Butch told them something that they really did not want to hear.

"Lt. Colonel Haung had all ministers killed many years ago." Butch said.

"I know of a Lieutenant Haung ... of many years ago but, not a Lt. Colonel Haung." Brandon mentioned.

"That's him." Butch said. "He got promoted a couple of times and then was put in charge of the Centerville area after chasing the Mountain Ghost into the north."

"He didn't ..." Jenifer said before being stopped by Brandon.

"What she means is that we have heard that the Mountain Ghost was coming back. Then again we've heard many things about him."

Jenifer caught herself and calmly said; "I also heard that he was dead."

"Maybe but I doubt it." Eve said. "I also heard that he was running for president of Free America."

The five of them continued to talk for many hours. As it started to get dark Brandon mentioned that they needed to find shelter for the night. That was when Eve invited them to their shack. "It is not very big but you can sleep on the floor. It isn't good to be out at night anymore."

"Why is that?" Ann asked.

"Because the drones that fly at night will kill anyone that is out after dark." Eve advised.

"The large drones right?" Brandon asked.

"No." Butch said. "They are about a foot and a half wide and black. You can't see them until it is to late."

"I heard that they could not see at night and therefore can't fly at night." Ann said.

"Oh that was a long time ago." Eve said. "They even had

pilots flying them back then."

"They don't have a Korean flying them anymore?" Brandon asked.

"No." Butch said. "They fly automatic now. Where are you three from?"

Brandon looked at the girls and then admitted that they were from Free America. Butch and Eve just looked at them and then Eve asked why they would come there.

Jenifer stepped up and said; We came to fight the Chinese and North Koreans."

"Why would you do that?" Butch asked.

Jenifer thought before speaking but still admitted; "Because the Mountain Ghost is our father."

"Is you father?" Eve asked.

"Yes." Ann said. He's still alive."

"Could you use a couple of more soldiers?" Butch asked. "We don't have any weapons but we will fight."

Brandon looked at the two girls and asked; "What do you think?"

"Do you know how to use a rifle?" Jenifer asked Butch and Eve.

"Until a few years ago we had a couple of Ak-47 rifles." Butch said. "But without any oil to keep them clean and lubricated they rusted out.

"They are completely useless now." Eve said.

Brandon looked at the girls and said; "I guess we'll need to find them a couple of rifles."

That night everyone slept well. To get Butch and Eve used to it Brandon had them stand watch that night with him standing the first watch. The Chinese and North Koreans in that area still did not know about the Ghost Warriors being there so there was nothing to really worry about.

When Brandon woke up it was almost daylight. He looked for who was on watch and found Eve sitting in a chair asleep. Instantly he jumped her about it scaring her out of the chair and onto the floor. Butch came in the den yelling at Brandon for yelling at Eve.

"Butch." Brandon tried to explain. "If a Korean patrol comes through here and we are all asleep then how would we survive?"

"I don't care." Butch yelled at Brandon. "You never yell at her."

Brandon looked at the twins and said; "We can't use them. She sleeps on watch and he has an attitude problem. They don't want to survive."

"I'll show you an attitude problem." Butch yelled as he grabbed Brandon.

Using the Ju-jitsu that his father taught all three of them Brandon grabbed Butch and threw him against the wall. As soon as Butch got up he ran at Brandon and got thrown against the wall again.

"I don't want to hurt you Butch." Brandon warned. "But I will if I have to."

This time when Butch got up he did not run at Brandon. "Where did you learn that?" he asked Brandon.

"From my father." he answered. "We have been trained from the age of three to come here and fight the North Koreans. Now if you want to join us then that's fine but you will fallow orders. If you can't do that then it's simple. We can't use you."

Butch thought for a few second and realized that he wanted to be able to fight the North Koreans more than anything. "I'm sorry Brandon. We can fallow orders."

Brandon looked at Eve and said; "You will not fall asleep on duty again will you?"

"No Sir." Eve replied.

"I may be in charge but we are family now." Brandon advised her. "You don't need to be calling me Sir."

After that the five talked for a while. After it got dark they left the shack and went to get the three rifles left out in the field. After retrieving their rifles they headed for Centerville where they hoped to get a couple of rifles for the new members of the Ghost Warriors.

Not knowing the area as well as their fathers did they

fallowed Highway 7 but stayed in the trees. After the first day they decided to continue traveling at night. They had forgotten about the drones. Butch had mentioned that the black drones now flew at night and they no longer had pilots. They flew automatically which meant that they could be anyplace at anytime. The black drones also killed people that were out at night but neither Butch nor Eve said how. *They must carry guns of some type*. Brandon thought.

Later Brandon asked Butch how the black drones killed people. When he mentioned some type of gun both Butch and Eve laughed.

"Sorry for laughing but that would make them to heavy to fly." Butch said. Then with a smile he said; "They carry small rockets and they are very accurate."

"Tell me about these rockets." Brandon said.

Still smiling Butch said; "The black drones carry four rockets that are about the size of a fifty caliber round. They explode on contact. Anyone that is hit by one of them usually dies.

This was a new threat that Russ and Wu did not have to deal with. It was going to be an all new war for the Ghost Warriors. It was a new war for their fathers and they did well. The Ghost Warriors would do well as well.

As the Ghost Warriors worked their way through the woods they came upon three Korean soldiers. The soldiers were very young and just stood there not sure of what they should do. Instantly Brandon, Jenifer, and Ann raised their rifles and captured the soldiers.

Jenifer and Ann tied the prisoners to three trees and then sat down with the others to decide what to do. Butch and Eve now had AK-47s. As they talked Brandon noticed that one of the prisoners was listening to their every word. He stood and walked over to the prisoner.

"You understand English?" Brandon asked.

"Oh yes." the prisoner said. "I was in officer's training where they taught me English."

"Why aren't you an officer?" Brandon asked.

"I failed only because I did not see things their way."

"What do you mean?"

"They taught us about the Mountain Ghost and how evil he was but I saw him as a great warrior." the prisoner said. "He might not have been one of us but he was still a brilliant fighter and strategist."

"What's your name?" Brandon asked.

"I am Leo." he said. "Leo Kim. I wish that I had been born about twenty years earlier."

"Why is that?"

"If I had been born twenty years ago I wound not be here about to die and ... I could have joined the Mountain Ghost and fought with him."

"Fight your own people?" Brandon asked.

About twenty years ago many of the North Korean soldiers turned against the Chinese and fought the Koreans that were loyal to them. I would have done it too."

Brandon stood and walked back to the others. Once he sat down he told them what all Leo had said. Even though they knew how he felt Butch and Eve were not willing to take a chance and be nice to him.

The next morning the Ghost Warriors decided to let the prisoners go so that they could tell the Chinese and North Koreans that they were there. When Butch and Eve untied the prisoners two of them knocked Butch and Eve to the ground and grabbed Eve's rifle. Leo grabbed Butch's rifle. When the other prisoner pointed his rifle at Brandon and yelled something in Korean Leo made a decision and fired at the soldier. Then he fired again leaving the other two Korean soldiers dead.

After quickly laying his rifle down he asked Brandon; "Have I proven myself?"

"Proven what?" Brandon asked.

As Leo slowly raised his hands and turned to face Brandon he said; "I want to join you. Like I told you I was born to late to join the Mountain Ghost but, I hope you will let me join you."

"Well he did save our lives when they could have all gotten away." Eve said.

"What do the rest of you think?" Brandon asked the others."

After everyone agreed Brandon also agreed. The Ghost Warriors now had six members. Then Brandon broke the news to Leo as to who Jenifer and Ann were. Leo walked over to the girls and kissed their hands. He might not have been able to fight with the Mountain Ghost but he would be able to fight with the daughters of the Mountain Ghost. That was good enough.

"You know…" Leo said. "… you should not let Chinese Command or especially Lt Colonel Haung know that you're here. Let them find out. There is no reason to have hundreds of our … Korean soldiers looking for you before you're ready."

"I know but we did not think about it that way." Brandon said. "I will be depending on your advise a great deal you know."

"I figured you would." Leo told him with a smile.

As the Ghost Warriors continued to walk Brandon told Leo how his grandfather and the first Mountain Ghost, met Sergeant Wu.

"Are you talking about the traitor … what the others call the Sergeant that betrayed his men over twenty five years ago?" Leo asked.

"He's the one." Brandon said. "He's in Dallas right now with my father."

"I would love to meet him some day." Leo said.

"You see Jenifer and Ann behind us?" Brandon asked Leo. "The Mountain Ghost is their father."

The more Leo learned the more respect he had for the group. Being a part of the Ghost Warriors gave him a great deal of pride. He slowed his walk so that the sisters could catch up with him. After talking to them for a while Leo found favor in Ann over her sister. Ann was stronger and he liked that. It was the only way to tell which sister was which.

The Ghost Warriors decided to attack the Patrol barracks

in Jewett. The Korean's first barracks had been destroyed many years earlier by Russ and the Ghost Soldiers. Rather than rebuild it the North Koreans used the old B & B grocery store. After moving all of the empty shelves outside there was plenty of room for offices and a barracks.

There were much more trees on the east side of Jewett so the Ghost Warriors had to move around the southern side of town and work their way up to the east side. It took a while but they finally reached the trees behind the barracks. Just as they walked up to the edge of the trees at the back of the barracks a truck pulled up.

The driver and passenger got out and walked into the barracks using the back door. Brandon told everyone to guard him as he looked in the back of the truck. Thinking that there were weapons that they could use he opened the back tarp. There were plenty of things to take but there were also six North Korean soldiers back there. Brandon quickly ran back into the trees but not where the others were. Just as he reached the trees two of the soldiers in the back of the truck jumped out and opened fire. Brandon was hit twice but he was still able to run.

The other five members of the Ghost Warriors ran deeper into the trees. The Korean soldiers did not see them. However the two soldiers that fired at Brandon took off after him. Brandon saw that he was leaving a blood trail. He had been hit in the side of the neck and in the side. Both bullets went in and came out the other side. After a few minutes Brandon turned south to go where they had crossed the southern side of town. Not knowing this, the soldiers continued to travel east.

The twins and the others were heading to the same area south of town where Brandon was heading when they saw the two Korean soldiers. With Jenifer being second in charge she stopped everyone. Not knowing exactly what was going on she did not want to fight. With only five of them and a barracks full of North Korean soldiers Jenifer had the others squat down so they would not be seen. Once the two soldiers pass they continued on their way.

Jenifer took the others south of town to wait until it got dark. They had to cross Highway 79 before going any farther. As they waited they saw many trucks loaded with North Korean soldiers passing them. Suddenly there was a sound behind them and they all whipped around to fire. Standing there was Brandon limping and leaning over.

Brandon had lost a great deal of blood but the twins worked to patch him up. The bullet that went into his side exited just a few inches away. This caused him to loose a great deal of blood but it looked like no organs were hit. There was no way that they could know for sure though. The bullet that passed through the side of his neck also exited an inch away not hitting anything bad. However he was loosing some blood there as well. The girls patched Brandon the best they could with what little in first aid gear they had and then had him lay still. That was no problem for Brandon.

By time it got dark enough to cross Highway 79 the constant passing of Korean trucks had stopped. Butch and Eve helped Brandon to his feet but he was already stiff. Every move he made was painful and was hard to do. The sisters went out to the edge of the trees and looked for anyone that might be coming. With no one in sight everyone stepped out onto the side of the road and crossed the highway.

The Ghost Warriors continued walking until Brandon could walk no more. Now in the trees southwest of town they felt safe in stopping for a while. By this time Brandon was gasping for air but there was nothing that any of them could do. Finally he took his last breath and slowly let it out. Brandon was dead. Jenifer and Ann started crying. They had know Brandon all their lives and had trained with him for the past seventeen years. He was like a brother to them. Using their knives Jenifer, Ann, and Leo began digging a shallow grave. Using their hands when they could Butch and Eve helped. By morning they had Brandon buried but he was not buried deep. Fearing that animals might dig his body up they all gathered some of the many iron ore rocks in the area and placed them on his grave. With it being daylight they left the area but stayed in the trees.

Their first big mission ended in the loss of their friend and leader. Jenifer was now in charge with Ann second in charge. Depression set into the twins but they knew that they could not let this failure bother them. Their father warned them that they would sometimes fail but they just did not expect their first failure to be their first mission. By that night the Ghost Warriors were tired and stopped to rest. That night they discuss what they would do next.

Chapter 2

The Guns

Loosing Brandon was not easy for Jenifer and Ann but they were dealing with it well. They would never forget him but they would be able to continue without him.

Leo and Ann stated getting along well. Before long they were doing things together. Jenifer was not sure if she liked them being together with him being a North Korean but their mother was Korean. It should not have mattered but, for some reason it did. Maybe it was because a few days earlier Leo was the enemy.

One day as the Ghost Warriors were hiding in the woods just east of Marquez they saw a Korean convoy stop for the night. In the convoy were four trucks, two of which were full of soldiers and the other two full of wooden crates, three trucks pulling trailers loaded with tanks and one North Korean ambulance with a medical team. While the others stayed in the woods Butch and Eve walked into town to talk to their old friends.

Butch and Eve learned that the tanks were going to Waco. They were suppose to be having a parade soon. As for the other vehicles they could learn nothing. Their friends did not know what the trucks were doing. They also learned that the depot farther to the west had been destroyed many years earlier by American jets but, it was now being rebuilt. Like the fuel depot in Centerville many years earlier the Chinese put the large tanks underground. They were doing the same with this depot. This time they were putting anti-aircraft guns around the area as well. This would give the Ghost Warriors many targets.

Later that night Butch and Eve met the others at their old home. It was a small shack but they made do. Butch and Eve told the others what they had learned. What they did after that was Jenifer's decision. Although she listened to the others her job as the group's leader was to make final decisions. For now they would rest and then they would recon the area around the fuel depot on Highway 7 just west of Marquez.

The Ghost Warriors were getting ready to leave Marquez and recon the area around the fuel depot when two North Korean companies drove into town. Within minutes the town of Marquez was full of over two hundred North Korean soldiers. Fearing that they were looking for the Ghost Warriors Jenifer had everyone fallow her away from town. Using the darkness of the night they headed for the trees a few hundred yards east of town. Once there they stopped and watched the show.

The Korean soldiers gathered everyone in town and had them stand in front of the old Exxon gas station. The civilians were doing nothing but standing around talking. Just over fifty American civilians were standing in front of the gas station when about fifty Korean soldiers were given the orders to open fire. For no reason at all the civilians were killed.

"That's Lieutenant Colonel Haung giving the orders." Eve said. "He's a nasty one ... very evil."

Jenifer and Ann looked hard at the Korean giving the orders to murder everyone. Their father had mentioned him so many times and said the same thing that Eve said. He was an evil one. Now that they got to see Haung they could put a face to all of the things their father said about him. The Ghost Warriors hid and stayed down in the trees and bushes the rest of the day and that night. Before morning the North Koreans had already moved out. Eve was on guard when they left but she had fallen asleep on watch again. She did not see where they went.

When Eve woke everyone up she got a serious butt chewing from Jenifer for falling asleep on duty again. This time Butch said nothing. When she finished with Eve she gave Butch a long look half way hoping he would say something this time. He looked deep into her eyes and said nothing.

Jenifer whipped around and grabbed her rifle. Then she

left the woods to walk way around Marquez in case some soldiers were still around. The others fallowed. As they walked Butch spoke to his wife but she thought that he was turning against her.

"Shut up woman." Butch yelled at Eve. "Your falling asleep on duty can get us all killed. I thought that you loved me but you must not."

"Shhhhhh!" Ann whispered. "You're the one that's about to get us killed."

Butch started to say something back to Ann but realized that she was right. After taking a deep breath and letting it out he continued to walk.

The Ghost Warriors crossed Highway 7 and stayed in the trees until they got about two miles north of Marquez. Then they crossed Highway 79 and headed to the west.

The depot was only about two miles west of the town of Marquez. It took two hours to come to the first anti-aircraft guns just north of the depot. It was a large gun with about twenty Korean soldiers guarding it. There were not enough Ghost Warriors to attack it. Jenifer sent Butch and Eve on to the west to learn more about anymore anti-aircraft guns. They would meet the next night in the trees north of Highway 7 and across from the depot. She sent Leo and Ann south across Highway 7 to recon south and west of the depot. Jenifer would spend her time watching the depot itself.

The depot had six guard towers; two at the gate. Because of the shape of the field the depot was built in the wire fence around the depot. It had five sides. There was a long building along the northeast fence and a larger building at the southern corner of the compound. Another smaller building that looked to be a barracks was located east of the larger building. A large area had been covered with concrete that stood about one foot above the ground. This probably covered the underground fuel tanks. Attacking this place was going to be impossible as well.

The next night Butch and Eve came in first. They watched an anti-aircraft gun west of the depot that looked like a carbon copy of the one to the north. Close to morning Leo and Ann came back with their report. They reported two more anti-aircraft guns; one east of the depot and another one to the south. All four anti-aircraft guns had about twenty or more Korean soldiers working and guarding it. Small clearings were cleared in the trees where the guns were placed making it impossible for American jets to find them. It looked like the Ghost Warriors would not be able to do anything about the depot.

The group rested that night and the next day as they took turns watching the depot. Trucks were coming in and out all day and most of the night. Crates that looked like weapons and ammunition were being unloaded from trucks and carried into the long warehouse on the northwest fence. Other trucks delivered smaller crates to the larger warehouse. Fuel trucks brought in fuel to the underground tanks. With all that they had seen going in the depot they still had no idea as to what was there. Finally Jenifer decided that the Ghost Warriors would have to hit an incoming convoy to see what was being brought in.

That night the group left the safety of the trees and headed east. Once they crossed Highway 79 they continued east for a couple of miles. By this time daylight was lighting up the area so the group stopped and rested. It would be there that the Ghost Warriors would make themselves known.

The Ghost Warriors lined up along Highway 7 to attack the first convoy that came along. Not knowing the convoy's schedule they set in for a long wait but, it would not be a long wait. Jenifer was the one that set up at the eastern end of their line. If she fired then the others would. They had only waited for about thirty minutes when trucks were seen coming towards them from Centerville. Most of these trucks came out of Houston and the port of Houston on Interstate 45 and turned west on Highway 7.

When Jenifer noticed that the convoy was heavily guarded she held her fire. However; Eve; thinking that she knew better opened fire. When the convoy came to a screeching halt the other Ghost Warriors had no idea as to what they should do.

"Run." Jenifer yelled out to the others.

The Ghost Warriors turned and ran away from the highway and the Korean soldiers. Deeper into the woods they ran as the soldiers started firing into the trees. When Jenifer had run a good half mile she stopped and turned to fight. Through the trees and yaupon brush she saw Ann and Leo running to her right. Jenifer yelled and they stopped. Then they also turned and got ready for a fight. The three of them waited for almost an hour before Jenifer crept over to Ann and Leo.

"What do you two think?" Jenifer asked.

"I think I heard the trucks drive off earlier." Leo advised.

"Okay then." Jenifer said. "Spread out and let's see if we can find Butch and Eve."

The three spread out about twenty feet apart and walked towards the convoy. As they walked slowly through the brush they saw no one. Finally they came to the highway but all of the trucks were gone. Then Leo yelled out to Jenifer and Ann.

"I found Butch."

In front of Leo was the body of their friend Butch. He had been shot five times in the chest and left there to rot. Eve was nowhere to be found.

"I guess Eve was captured." Leo advised.

"I don't trust her." Ann said. "She's a bad apple and caused all of this."

"I know." Jenifer replied. "But … she's still one of us."

"We need to start getting more selective of who we let into our group." Ann said with a bit of anger.

"We should bury Butch before we leave." Jenifer said.

"No!" Leo argued. "If they come back and see him gone they will know that others were with him."

"Okay then … let's go." Jenifer ordered.

The Ghost Warriors got nothing accomplished and lost two members in the process. Now they were back down to just the three of them. The only thing that they did accomplish was the recon of the depot. Even when there were five of them they could not have attacked any part of the depot or the guns around it. Now with just three of them there was no way that they could do anything.

The Ghost Warriors went back into the woods to rest and decide on what they were to do next. As the three sat against trees to rest they heard explosions off to the west.

"That's about where the depot is." Ann suggested.

A few seconds later American jet flew over with Chinese MIG fighter jets behind them. An air battle started. Seven Chinese MIG fighters were fighting five American fighters. Within a few seconds three of the MIGs had already been shot down and all five American jets were still in the fight. Just before the Chinese MIGs turned to go back home one of them shot down an American jet. It crashed about a quarter of a mile from the Ghost Warriors. They decided to try to make it to the pilot before the North Koreans did. Hopefully the pilot was still alive.

Because of the thick brush it took the Ghost Warriors almost an hour to get to the crash site. The pilot must have been knocked out. He was just crawling out of the cockpit when the Ghost Warriors ran up to him. Only knowing that someone had just run up to him the pilot fell to the ground expecting to be shot.

"Can you run?" Jenifer yelled as she grabbed his flight jacket. "Answer me. Can you run?"

"Yes." the pilot said as Jenifer pulled him to his feet.

The four of them ran for a good mile before the pilot collapsed. Figuring that they were far enough from the crash site Jenifer sent Ann and Leo back a little ways to watch for anyone coming at them.

"Who are you?" Jenifer got right to the point.

"I'm Second Lieutenant David Parker of the American Air Force, Seventh Wing. He said. "Who the hell are all of you?"

"Friends." Jenifer said as she waved for Ann and Leo to come in. "That's all you need to know for now."

When David saw Leo running in wearing his North Korean uniform and carrying an AK-47 he backed up. Then he realized that this North Korean was with the two girls.

"My name is Leo." Leo told David as he stuck out his hand. "Yes I'm your friends too."

David took in a deep breath and let it out as he shook Leo's hand. "Okay."

"Okay David." Jenifer said. "Tell us a little about you."

David went on to tell the others that he was with the Seventh Wing of the American Air Force out of Dallas. They were taking anyone that could fly a kite and trained them to fly the jets. Then the pilot was given the rank of Second Lieutenant before flying out on their first mission.

"So you have had no officer training?" Jenifer asked.

"None what so ever." David replied.

"Well I'm in charge here." Jenifer quickly informed David. "As long as you are with us you will fallow my orders."

"I have no problem with that." David replied again.

"We'll get you a rifle as soon as we can." Jenifer said as she looked over the newest member of the group. "How old are you?"

"I'm twenty one." David said with a smile. "How old are you?"

"I'm eighteen but I still give the orders here." Jenifer said as she tried to downplay his advances. "Lets get out of here."

Jenifer stood and walked off with Ann and Leo behind her. David stood and took up the rear. For the time being he carried a 38 caliber revolver pistol. If they got into any firefight with any North Korean soldiers he would only have six shots. He wanted a rifle in a bad way. The Ghost Warriors headed back to the west and to the northern anti-aircraft guns.

Two nights later they were standing in the trees across a large field from the northern anti-aircraft guns. Leaving Leo at the edge of the trees to watch the guns the others retreated back into the trees. Jenifer decided to watch the northern guns for a while and get some rest. Jenifer told David about Butch and Eve and her goal to grow in membership in the Ghost Warriors.

"So … you're the Ghost Warriors?" David asked. "Everyone in Dallas has heard of you."

"How is that?" Ann asked. "We haven't been here long enough to do anything."

"Of course ... your Jenifer and your Ann."

"How do you know us?" Jenifer asked.

"The Mountain Ghost is your father." David said with a big smile. "He came into one of our classes in pilot school and told us about what all he did. Then he told us about you two."

"Dad's talking about us again." Ann calmly told Jenifer.

"Oh he said nothing bad about either of you." David assured them. "He's so proud of you two ..."

"We were joking David." Ann said as she stood and walked off to Leo. Then she stopped and looked back at her sister. "I like him Sis. Maybe we should get him a rifle."

"What did she mean ... she liked me?"

"Anyone coming into our group has to be voted in by the other members." she told David. "She just gave her vote."

"And you?"

"I'll vote yes but you need the votes of all three of us."

"So my membership in your group depends on the vote of a North Korean soldier?" David asked.

"Keep this in mind while you wait for that vote. Leo is from North Korea but he is no longer a North Korean soldier. He is one of us." Jenifer said in a very rude way. "You will except that or you will not get my vote. It's that simple."

At that time Leo walked into the camp. Jenifer asked him to cast a vote on David joining them. Leo instantly agreed to it. Jenifer looked at David.

"That issue we were talking about." Jenifer said as she looked into his eyes. "Where do you stand?"

"If you trust him then I will. I have no problem with it." David said with a straight face.

"Then it looks like your in." Jenifer said with a smile. She shook David's hand and advised him that they were a family and he was now part of that family.

As Leo and Jenifer lay down to get some sleep David leaned against a tree and thought about what he was getting into. The main thing on his mind was that he was single and only three years older than Jenifer. She was a beautiful woman; a woman that any man would kill for. Leo had already made it known that Ann was his woman leaving only Jenifer. But David did not know how she felt about him. First he had to prove himself to the group; his new family. He would worry about having a new girlfriend later.

Eve had been taken directly to the jail in Centerville. For the first four days she was in a cell all by herself. Then one morning she was taken to an office and forced into a chair. Behind her were the two North Korean soldiers that brought her there. In front of her was a large wooden desk. She started to ask the soldiers why she was there but the soldier to her right reached around and slapped her.

"Shut ... up." the soldier told her.

A few minutes later the door to the office opened and closed. Then she could hear someone whispering to the two soldiers but she did not speak Korean and had no idea as to what was said. Finally a Chinese officer walked around and sat on the other side of the desk.

"I am Lieutenant Colonel Haung ... Commanding officer of all Chinese and North Korean forces in this area. Who are you?" Haung was being very polite.

"My name is Eve."

"There's no need to be scared Eve." Haung said. "I am only seeing you right now because you are about to be executed for having a rifle and for firing at some of my soldiers."

"I didn't fire at anyone." Eve pleaded.

"I know you didn't." Haung said. "Some of the soldiers on that convoy said that your friends fired and then left you and ... that other man there to be captured. He was killed.

"He was my husband." she replied.

"I'm sorry to hear that." Haung said with a kind voice. But you can still be executed for having a rifle with you anyway. However ... I am sure you can be saved from that."

Eve was quiet for a moment and then asked; "What do you want?"

"All you have to do is tell me who these people that you

were with are and I will call off your execution. It's not like they are your friends. They left you and ... your husband there to die and be captured."

Eve continued to be quiet for a while as Haung continued to talk. He told her things that only she should have known. Facing death in a few minutes she finally had, had enough and yelled out.

"All right." Eve said. "I'll tell you what I know but just shut up."

"For one thing don't tell me to shut up." Haung said through his grinding teeth. "And second of all ... tell me what you know."

Eve did not want to die but she did not want to spend the rest of her life in prison either. "What could I do to keep me from prison the rest of my life?"

"I can only promise you that if you tell me what I want you'll not be executed." Haung assured her. "Maybe we can ... work something out after we talk."

Eve did not like what Haung was suggesting but she would not die either. She started talking and when she mentioned that Jenifer and Ann were the daughters of the Mountain Ghost he got excited.

"The Mountain Ghost?" he asked Eve.

"Yes Sir." Eve agreed. "They're his two daughters."

Haung smiled and began to form a plan. He never could catch his old enemy but maybe he can capture his enemy's children. Letting the Mountain Ghost know that he had his two little girls might bring him back down to fight again.

"What else do you know about these two girls?" Haung asked Eve.

"That's it Sir." Eve replied. "I ... my husband and I were not with them long."

"Well Eve ... you saved yourself from that nasty execution." Haung. "I'll talk to you within the next few days about ... the rest of your life."

"Thank you ..." Eve said before being interrupted.

"Get her out'a here." Haung ordered the two soldiers.

Haung smiled as Eve was taken away but his mind was not on her. He was thinking about the Mountain Ghost and his two precious little girls. Why were they there? Did they have ideas of continuing their father's dreams? He had no answers to these questions but he did know that there were only three of them. Haung did not know about David.

Instantly Haung sent out a squad of North Korean soldiers to where they had captured Eve. Their job was to find out where Jenifer and Ann had gone and report back to him. The squad got to the area late in the evening and setup camp. They knew where they were when they found Butch's body. The entire squad disappeared into the woods with only a couple of them standing guard just inside the trees along the highway.

The next morning the squad found footprints leading from what looked like a campsite used by more than just two people. The tracks showed that they headed towards Marquez. Fearing that then Ghost Warriors were heading to the depot their Sergeant called Haung on his radio and told him what the squad had found.

Haung had the Sergeant hold his squad there and wait for the rest of the company. Then they would be transported to the depot. Two hours later the rest of the company arrived. When the squad had loaded into the trucks the entire company left for the depot.

The Ghost Warriors had no idea that Eve had betrayed them and that one hundred and twenty North Korean soldiers were now at the depot looking for them. Only six North Korean soldiers manned the northern anti-aircraft guns so it looked like they could take it. A sudden and quick hit should do it. But what would they do then? They had no explosives and none of them knew how to make IEDs from the larger anti-aircraft shells. They would only be able to kill the soldiers and that would be it.

Jenifer decided that it would at least be a good hit to kill the soldiers but the Koreans would surely add soldiers to all of the gun emplacements after that. However; when the Ghost Warriors got into position to make their attack they found an entire platoon of North Korean soldiers there. For some reason about thirty soldiers were protecting the northern anti-aircraft guns There were now to many for just the four Ghost Warriors to attack. None of them would survive.

The Ghost Warriors retreated back to the trees where they had spent the last couple of nights. Once back at their makeshift camp the four of them sat down to make new plans.

Not finding the Ghost Warriors at or close to the depot Haung had the company of soldiers split up so that a platoon covered and protected the anti-aircraft guns. The remaining soldiers protected the depot itself. The added soldiers at the gun sites also made regular patrols around their gun sites. One of these patrols spotted the Ghost Warriors. Luckily, Dave also spotted them. The Ghost Warriors were able to leave the area before the patrol got to them.

A four man fire team was sent to fallow the Ghost Warriors while the others returned to the northern gun site. Tracks showed the fire team which way the Ghost Warriors went but at that time they were not sure that they were the Ghost Warriors. They thought that the Ghost Warriors only had the twin sisters not four people.

The Ghost Warriors headed to an area about three miles north of Marquez and crossed Highway 79 there. Then with it being dark and seeing no one of the highway they headed towards Jewett. A few miles later they saw headlights coming towards them and they went back into the trees on the eastern side of the highway. From there they went into the trees a bit more and sat down to rest. At daybreak they would move east again with no plan in mind.

When the North Korean fire team reached Highway 79 they could find no tracks on the eastern side. The Sergeant knew that the group they were fallowing had to have headed north or south on the highway but they found nothing that showed which way. He Sergeant figured that heading back to Marquez would be dangerous so they had to have headed towards Jewett. The fire team headed north.

The next morning came and the rising sun showed the fire

team where the group had left the highway and walked off into the trees on the eastern side. The fire team had been pushing all night without any rest so they were very tired. The Sergeant continued pushing his team but, as they cleared the eastern side of the trees they came to a large field. On the other side of the field were four people still about one hundred yards from the safety of the trees on the other side.

The Sergeant had his team open fire on the group. One of his men had a sniper's rifle and fired. When the Ghost Warriors heard the shooting behind them they ran into the trees. Just before getting into the trees enough that the trees would stop any bullets David was hit in the lower back. He instantly went down. Jenifer set up an ambush using David as the bait.

As soon as the fire team came into the trees they gathered around David. As they laughed the small group took aim and opened fire. Within seconds the North Korean fire team was dead. The first thing that Jenifer did was grab an AK-47 and hand it to David. Leo and Ann gathered everything the fire team had that was usable. After handing David his new rifle she looked at his wound.

"Your lucky you were shot with a North Korean bullet." Jenifer said to David. "They make their ammo cheep. There was not enough power in that shell to push through you."

Jenifer was able to pull out the bullet with her fingers and handed it to David. He was not bleeding real bad but bad enough. She put a patch over the wound and taped it down. Then she ordered Ann and Leo to stand guard. David would not be able to be moved for a few days.

Ann and Leo had to move the bodies of the fire team because David could not be moved for a few days and the stench of rotting flesh would not be very pleasant. They covered the bodies with dead tree limbs and leaves. The cold weather would slow the decaying of the fire team but Jenifer did not know how long they would be there.

After not hearing from the fire team for two days Haung sent out a few black drones to search the area where they were last known to be. On that day Ann saw two of these drones flying by close to their camp. Luckily the group was in the midst of thick yaupon brush and the drones could not fly to close. If they could just keep down until David could move then they might make it out of there.

During the past two days Jenifer had used up all of the gauze and most of the tape. When a black drone flew past their camp closer than they had before she made up her mind that they had to get out of there that night. When it got dark Jenifer and Ann helped David up. It was a bit painful but he stood. After a few steps David said that he could make it. He also knew that they needed to get out of the area. Jenifer took the lead with David behind her.

Every few steps David felt a sharp pain in his lower back that almost sent him to his knees but, he stayed up. Before long they were out of the immediate area. They had to stop every now and then to let David rest but they got away. By time the eastern sky was turning blue they had traveled only one mile and found themselves in a large area of trees. Jenifer ordered the others to set up camp. As usual; there would be no campfire that night.

Chapter 3

Lieutenant Bakers

It was another week before the Ghost Warriors moved on. David's back was doing well as the bullet did not touch his back bone or spinal column. Jenifer credited God for the bullet stopping just under the skin but she also blamed it on the cheep ammunition that the North Koreans made for their military. David still could not stand for a long time but at least he was able to walk short distances.

The Ghost Warriors were in a large group of oak trees about half way between Jewett and Marquez. They still had no plans but Jenifer was waiting until David was much better than he was. There was still just the four of them.

Jenifer's desire to recruit others into the Ghost Warriors had not gone as well as she thought it would. One of the problems that she had was their membership growing only to be cut back down to size. Another problem was that they ran into very few people that they could trust or anyone that wanted to join them. She and Ann wanted nothing more than to fallow their father's dream; their dream now. Their father did many things alone and with his friend Wu but it was a much different war now.

The Ghost Warriors had to face automated black drones that flew during the day and night. Unlike their father they had large drones that now had infer red cameras that could tell the difference between a rodent and human during the night. The large drones carried four bombs each and the black drones carried four tiny rockets. Fighting this resistance was not as easy as it was when their father was doing it.

One morning Jenifer looked out over a field and saw a black drone slowly flying just above the ground. "You guys ready to move out?" she asked the others.

Upon their agreeing to move out Jenifer took aim at the drone with her father's 270 rifle and fired. She missed but the drone did not hear the bullet whizzing by and continued. She took aim again and this time sent the drone to the ground. Then she lead the others to the downed black drone where she picked it up and looked into the camera. Hoping that her image and voice was being recorded she yelled into the camera.

"My name is Jenifer Blake; one of the daughters of the Mountain Ghost. Just wanted to let you know that we are here to pick up where our father left off. This means that we are looking for you Haung ... and we will find and kill you."

God help us. I've let them know about us now so we will be needing your help Father. Please be with us and help the Ghost Warriors to grow ... with people that we can trust. Please send them to us Father.

Jenifer did not know for sure but she got her wish. A North Korean pilot is always behind the controls of five black drones. One of these pilots recorded Jenifer and what she said. Within an hour Lieutenant Colonel Haung was looking at the recording. His anger almost raged to the point of scaring the soldiers around him. Then he stood and took a deep breath.

"Find them. Use what ever you need to but find them." Haung ordered through his teeth. "I want them alive."

The soldiers left the office not sure what they should do. The corporal that served as Haung's secretary asked what he needed. Haung stood silent for a few seconds and had the corporal call Lieutenant Lee who worked under Captain Zing at the jail. Although Lee was a Chinese name he was still considered as North Korean because he was raised there.

An hour later there was a knock on Haung's office door. Lieutenant Lee walked in and saluted Haung. He stood tall and proud and was a shining example of an officer.

"I need some help Lieutenant." Haung said as he looked at Lee. "I need a man that ... has your qualifications."

"May I ask what qualifications you are talking about Sir?"

Lee asked.

"Your kind of like me ... in a way. Haung said with a smile. "You hated the Mountain Ghost when you were young ... didn't you."

"Yes Sir." Lee quickly answered. "He killed my father."

"How would you like to be put in charge of a platoon of soldiers that did nothing but try to capture ... and I mean capture ... the twin daughters of the Mountain Ghost?"

Lee smiled. "I would love that Sir."

"Good ... then you take the office beside mine." Haung said. "You and I will be working together but, you will be in the field more than you will be here. Move your things into that office and I will get you your platoon."

"I would rather have two squads Sir." Lee suggested. A smaller group is easier to control and less likely to be seen."

"I'll give you a platoon and you can do what you want with them." Haung insisted.

"Thank you Sir." Lee agreed as he turned to leave.

"Oh by the way." Haung said. "You are now a Captain."

""Thank you Sir."

"Just find them or you will be a lieutenant again." Haung advised.

"I understand Sir." Lee said as he left the office.

One day while scavenging for food Ann came upon a child playing in her the back yard. Stopping at the edge of the trees she hoped that the child did not see her. But the little girl looked up and looked right at her.

"Mom." the girl yelled.

A woman came outside and instantly saw Ann standing there with her rifle. "Please don't hurt us." the woman pleaded as she grabbed her daughter.

"I'm not gon'a hurt anyone ma'am." Ann let her know.

After talking for a few minutes the woman invited Ann into her home. The woman's name was Britney Barns and her daughter was Susan. Her husband, Mike, was out checking traps. They had been chased out of their home by a North Korean patrol two years earlier and moved into this home after finding it. No one claimed ownership so they did.

Ann told Britney about their group and how David had been badly hurt. Britney instantly asked Ann to bring David to their home and out of the cold. Ann thought for a while and agreed.

When Ann got back to the others she told Jenifer about the woman and her offer. Jenifer was scared to trust anyone but David did need to be in a place where it was warm. The wet and cold was hurting him and probably causing his back to heal slower. She agreed and the others fallowed her to the woman's home.

By time the group got back to the home Mike had come back from checking his traps. Mike and Britney were young; about twenty seven years old. Susan was six. When the group walked up to the home Mike came out. He wanted to meet the people that his wife invited to stay with them for a while. He did not like Leo especially as he still wore the North Korean uniform but excepted him along with the others.

After laying a few blankets on the floor in front of the fireplace they helped David to lay down. Another blanket served as his pillow. His bandages were removed and his wound cleaned. Then Britney used some of their gauze and tape to patch him back up. Then they gently turned his back towards the fire to keep it warm.

"He'll be okay." Mike said. "My wife used to be a nurse."

"That's good to hear." Ann said as she sat on the couch.

Mike had caught a fox in one of his snares and went back outside to skin and clean it. They would eat well that night. After the invasion of the Chinese and North Koreans any food at all was taken advantage of. Many Americans died the first two years from not having anything to eat; many of those because they would not eat some animals. Choosing to starve to death only because you would not eat a mouse or other animals is stupid. Meat is meat and it is all edible. Now plants are another story.

That evening Britney roasted the fox over the fire in the fireplace. Mike had redesigned the fireplace to double as a place to cook by using the iron ore rocks found in the area. He even decorated the front of it with some petrified wood also found in the area. There was also coalmines in the area with veins of coal running all over the place. Where ever the coal touched the petrified wood it caused crystals to form on the petrified wood itself. Mike had done a great job. Their fireplace was beautiful.

That night they all ate well. Roasted fox and sweet potatoes from the garden left everyone full. Jenifer offered their services as hunters as long as they were allowed to stay. Mike and Britney graciously excepted. The fox they were eating was the best catch Mike had made in about three months.

One morning Leo was out hunting with Jenifer's 270 rifle when he came upon three North Korean soldiers. They had been given permission to have three days off to go hunting. Leo walked right upon them almost getting shot for it. When the three soldiers saw that Leo was wearing a North Korean uniform they lowered their rifles. They thought that Leo was also hunting so, he allowed them to think that. He even went back to their camp with them in hopes of learning as much as he could.

The four of them talked for a long time until the soldiers started turning in for the night. They offered Leo a chance to spend the night in their camp but he said that he had to get back to his own camp. He said that hunting hogs and wolves was best done at night. He knew that those were the two most feared animals by the Chinese and North Korean soldiers and he hoped that they would want nothing to do with his hunt. He was right.

Finding his way back to the home during the night was impossible. After coming across a small stream he stopped for the night. Being alone and wearing a North Korean uniform he had no problem starting a campfire. Later that night a black drone seemed to drop from the treetops and hover a few feet in front of him. It scared him but then realized that anyone watching that camera would only see a North Korean soldier. He waved at the drone which swayed left and then right, waving back. Then it took off and flew away.

Leo laughed at the drone and then put his campfire out. He did not want anyone to recognize him and come back. Hopefully the drone would not be able to came back to his camp without his fire showing it the way. Leo was right about the drone. All through the night he could hear the black drone flying around. By morning he had, had enough of the drone looking for him and left long before daylight.

Had someone recognize him on the drone video? He was sure that they thought that he was dead but now did they know he was alive? Did he mess things up by not worrying about the fire? Leo had no answers to these questions and only wanted to get out of the area as quickly as possible. However; he figured that maybe he should not go back to the home. What if a large drone or a black drone close by was watching him? He knew where the home was but headed the opposite direction.

After Leo had not shown up back at the home by morning Jenifer went looking for him. Since he carried her 270 rifle for hunting she had his AK-47. She felt very uncomfortable without her father's 270 in her hands. After about three hours she came upon the North Korean's camp but no one was there. The only way she knew that North Korean soldiers had been there was because one of them had left the wrapper to one of their MREs.

She looked around but Leo wore the same boots that the soldiers wore. She had no idea if he had been there. Then she saw boot prints of one man that headed out of the camp and away from Mike and Britney's home. Boot prints from three other men lead off away from the ghost Warriors but at another direction than the other one.

Jenifer fallowed the tracks of the single man until it was late in the evening. Who ever wore those boots were going away from the Ghost Warrior's. Jenifer finally got back to the camp just after dark and told the others what she had found. Were the boots of the single soldier those of their friend Leo? Was he leading the other North Korean soldiers away from the Ghost Warriors in case they fallowed him? Where they fallowing him?

Not being sure if the three North Korean soldiers were fallowing Leo or not Jenifer decided to move out that night. David would stay there until the Ghost Twins got back. They would recon the eastern anti-aircraft guns just south of Highway 7. By time the sun was coming up they were on the eastern side of Highway 79. With the sun coming up and North Korean traffic increasing on the highway they rested in a small bunch of trees until that night.

While the twin sisters were working their way to the eastern anti-aircraft guns Leo showed back up at the house of Mike and Britney. As he walked up to the back door of the home Mike came out with a spear and almost ran Leo through. Just before stabbing Leo, Mike recognized him.

"Oh ... sorry man." Mike said as he quickly raised the knife that he had taped to the end of a stick. "All I saw was the uniform and no one else around."

It took a few seconds before Leo's heart started beating again. "I can make that spear a better one if you want." Leo offered.

After going into the home he learned that Jenifer and Ann had gone to recon the eastern guns. He checked on David who was sitting at the dinner table playing Uno with Britney. Then he went out to the garage with Mike and found things to make a better spear. After about thirty minutes Leo had a solid spear for mike. Then he added some hot tar from a bucket in the garage. By morning the tar had cooled into a hard cover over the wire holding the knife on the end of the six foot long tree limb.

When Leo got up the next morning he was thinking about trying to find Jenifer and Ann but Jenifer had left word for him if he returned. He was to stay there with David until she and Ann got back. With the last meat eaten in that home being a fox two days earlier Leo decided to go hunting again.

The eastern anti-aircraft guns were located beside a small group of trees but, for almost a quarter of a mile around it were large fields. The only place where Jenifer and Ann could hide and watch the guns was a small group of trees just south of the guns. The twins waited until nightfall and then slowly crawled across the fields and into the trees.

The small group if oak trees was also covered with thick yaupon brush and small cedar trees. It was a perfect place to recon the guns as long as a soldier did not want to walk through the group of trees. The only time they had to worry about being spotted that night was when a black drone flew by slow. The morning daylight brought on another threat.

Every hour a squad of North Korean soldiers would make rounds around the guns. They made a circle about two hundred yards around the guns bringing them right by the small group of trees where Jenifer and Ann were. Every time the squad came by which ever one of the twins was watching the guns would have to move back into the cover of the thick brush. A couple of times one of the soldiers would stop and look as deep into the brush as he could but saw no one and moved on.

Ann noticed that when the squad was making their rounds that left only three soldiers at the guns. When American jets flew close by the three soldiers were all that was needed to load and fire the anti-aircraft guns. If they had any explosives then they could attack the three soldiers while the squad was out and blow up the guns. This would have to be done before the squad could run back. But there was that same problem. They had no explosives.

That night Jenifer and Ann left the trees and crawled across the fields to more trees much farther from the eastern guns. With a few hours of darkness left they continued to make their way to Highway 79. They fallowed Highway 7 a few miles and then turned north and crossed it. Around noon the next day they walked up to the back door of Mike and Britney's home.

Just as Jenifer and Ann started to step inside the home Leo and Mike walked up carrying parts to a deer. They carried the meat into the kitchen where Britney helped them clean the meat.

David was doing very well. Two days later he and Jenifer went hunting. He needed to test how far he could push himself. That night they pitched a camp without a fire. David took the first watch. Being tired he fell asleep during his watch. Someone worked their way behind him and put a knife to his throat. David flinched but moved no more.

"It's real simple. Make a sound and I'll slit your throat." the man holding the knife said.

Three others walked up to Jenifer who was also sound asleep and gently kicked her in the shoulder. "Come up with a gun and you're dead." one of them said.

Jenifer and David were stood to their feet. Then a voice asked; "Jenifer? Jenifer Blake?"

"Yes Sir." she replied.

"Well dad gum ... it is you." one of the man said as he pulled off the black handkerchief covering his face.

"Lieutenant Bakers?" Jenifer asked with a smile.

"Actually it's First Lieutenant Bakers now." Bakers said. "I have three companies out here and we're getting ready to recon the anti-aircraft guns west of Marquez."

"Well actually ... we've already done that but our small group could never attack them."

"To many?"

"Yeah." Jenifer said. "They have twelve at all times and a squad makes rounds around the guns once an hour leaving only three with the guns."

Bakers looked around. "Where's your sister?"

We made some friends and she is there ... at their home." she replied.

"Who's this?" baker asked as he pointed at David.

"Oh he's one of us." she told Bakers.

Bakers looked at David and said; "You can put your hands down Son."

Jenifer, David, Bakers, and his men went to the home where the others were. Bakers' men scattered throughout the woods near the home and made sure there were no campfires. Jenifer, David, and Bakers went into the home and discussed what all the Ghost Warriors had learned.

Suddenly Bakers stopped their talking and asked Jenifer; "When was the last time you heard anything from home ... from your parents?"

"My god ... when we left." Then she knew that something was wrong. "Why?"

Bakers looked down and then back up at her. "Your father and mother are dead." Bakers sat back in his chair and added; "There were three of them. Two wore body bombs and one surrendered. His job was to deliver a message to you two."

"What happened?" Ann asked as Leo stood and she sat in his chair.

The two of them went into a building where your parents were and when they were close to them they blew themselves and ... your parents ... up. Then the other one surrendered and kept yelling in English that he had a message for the Mountain Ghost's twin girls."

For a while neither Jenifer nor Ann said anything. Then Jenifer asked what the message was.

"Lieutenant Colonel Haung wanted you two to know that he sent the two bombers so ... he killed your parents." Bakers said.

"What else?" Ann barely muttered.

"That's all. Haung just wanted you two to know that he killed them." Bakers said. "Now don't you two go hog wild and run into some trap because I am sure he has set one ... if not many for you. Calm down a while first and then plan an attack. Do not go into Centerville. He'll be waiting for you there."

Jenifer and Ann walked outside crying. They held each other and continued to cry for almost an hour. The others left the two girls alone so they could greave. David safely tucked the girl's rifles in the back room so they would not be tempted to do something stupid.

When the girls felt better they came back inside. Jenifer asked Bakers if she could show him the gun emplacements and he agreed. Ann would also go and take some of Bakers' men to the western and southern guns. Jenifer would show Bakers and a couple of his men the eastern and northern guns. That night the group left out to recon the anti-aircraft guns.

The remainder of Bakers' men stayed in the woods behind Mike and Britney's home. They did very little hunting; only when they had to eat. They did not bother anyone at the home.

Leo and David continued to help Mike and Britney all they could. David's back still hurt when he tried to chop wood so Leo cut and chopped all of the firewood. David was able to hunt so he did it to the south where Bakers' men were not around. One evening the three North Korean soldiers that Leo had met days earlier saw him in the woods and fallowed him to the house. Just as he started to step in the back door one of the North Korean soldiers yelled.

Leo quickly turned and saw the three Korean soldiers spread out and ready to fight. Leo asked what was going on and loud enough that everyone in the home could hear. Some of the American soldiers also heard him. When some of them stepped out of the woods the three Korean soldiers raised their rifles. From that moment on everything moved in slow motion.

Leo jerked his rifle up and started firing before it was even leveled at the Korean soldiers. The three Korean soldiers started firing at the American soldiers who walked out of the woods not expecting a fight. All four of the American soldiers were hit but Leo got all three of the North Korean soldiers. The entire fight only lasted about three seconds. All three of the North Korean soldiers were dead. Leo ran to check the American soldiers but got shot before he could get to them. Other American soldiers hearing the gunfire ran to their friend's aid and thought that Leo was one of the enemy.

Leo and one of the four American soldiers were carried into the home and laid on the den floor. The other three American soldiers were dead. With the home now full of American soldiers some of them picked up their friend and lay him on the kitchen table. David and Mike were the only ones tending to Leo.

"What are you doing?" one of the Americans asked Mike

and David. Take care of my man first ... before that ..."

"Shut up Sergeant." Britney yelled. "That Korean is one of us. "Do you hear me ... BOY?"

The Sergeant pulled back his head and went back to his man on the table. A few minutes later three men ran in. They were Bakers' medical team. Instantly they started working on the American soldier but, he was two far gone.

"Now get Leo up here." Britney yelled. None of them moved to help Leo. "If I have to tell Bakers that you refused to help Leo I'll make sure he scalps all of you ... and if he won't do it then I will. Anyone want to try me?"

"No Ma'am." one of the soldiers said barely above a whisper.

As the American soldiers started lifting Leo to lay him on the table Mike could only stare at his wife. This was a side of her that he had never seen before. Even Susan stood beside her dad just staring at her mom.

"He's one of us now." Britney yelled at the medical team. "Now do your magic for him or so help me God ..."

Leo had been hit one time in the side of the chest. The bullet shattered a rib but came out the other side. About three inches of the rib was nothing but bloody chips. The medical team removed the chips and patched Leo up. Then some of the American soldiers carried him to his cot. Then they moved the cot closer to the fireplace. Once the American soldiers learned that it was Leo that killed the three North Korean soldiers they started to like him. Many of them had met other North Korean soldiers that had deserted to the American side but this was the first time that they saw one North Korean soldier kill another.

No one slept that night except Leo who was out ever since he got shot. The American soldiers buried the other North Korean soldiers and their friends that also died. By morning the only hint that anything had happened was Leo laying on his cot.

"By the way ma'am." the Sergeant said to Britney. "I'm sorry about last night. We all saw that man wearing a North Korean uniform and ... well ... it's hard to break the habit and start caring for ... one of them. It's hard to not hate someone wearing that uniform."

Britney put her hand on the Sergeant's shoulder. "It's okay Sarg." she told him with a smile. "My husband and I almost killed him too."

"By the way Ma'am ... the name is Sergeant Myers." he said before walking back outside to his men.

Myers made sure that all of the other American soldiers knew who Leo was. Many of them had killed North Koreans for a long time and being nice to one was not natural. Knowing that he might have problems with some of them Myers ordered all of them to stay clear of the house. Then he talked to the other two sergeants and they agreed.

Three days later Jenifer and the others returned to the home. They sat at the dinner table and talked about everything that had happened. Jenifer, Ann, and Bakers told the others what they had learned about the anti-aircraft guns. Bakers had explosives and was going to use his men to attack the guns all at onetime. Then the plan was to move in and attack the depot.

Leo rolled over and asked what he could do but then he started laughing. Then the others realized that he was joking and also laughed. Bakers and Jenifer walked over to Leo. He had just woke up. He did not know that the four American soldiers were dead. He was actually pleased that he killed the three North Korean soldiers.

"I want to thank you for what you did." Bakers said to Leo. "Killing your own people can not possibly be very easy."

"As far as I'm concerned Sir ..." Leo said as he rolled over more. "I am an American. There are many of us that are tired of this war. My own government killed most of my family including my parents so ... I owe them nothing."

Ann walked over and sat on the floor by Leo's head. "I'm proud of him."

Bakers looked down at Ann and said; "I am to Ma'am. I am too."

Everyone was so wired up that it was very late in the morning before anyone started slipping away to get some sleep.

Ann pulled her cot over beside Leo and fell asleep holding his hand. When David lay on his cot Jenifer pulled her cot beside his.

"Do you care if I sleep here?" she asked him.

"Not at all." he said. "Not at all."

David and Jenifer talked for a while and just as he fell asleep she slowly slid her hand around him and fell asleep as well.

As Mike and Britney walked by the two couples to their bedroom they stopped. "Remember those days?" Mike asked his wife. Then they continued into their bedroom. Mike quietly closed the door and no one heard the turn of the lock.

Bakers sat alone at the table and said to himself. *I miss my wife.*

Chapter 4

The Depot

The next morning Mike got up to find that Leo was already up and had made coffee. "Coffee is made if you want some ... North Korean coffee." he told Mike.

"It's to early to laugh but catch me later." Mike advised the smiling man at the table. As they talked Ann got up and got her a cup of the coffee. She sat her cup on the table and then sat in Leo's lap. With her left arm around Leo's neck she reached out and picked up her coffee.

It did not take long for the conversation to start about the anti-aircraft guns. It did not matter what they talked about and thought that they had decided. Bakers was not there. He was the man that decided what would be done and how it would be done. It was a good three hours later before Bakers walked in the back door and into the kitchen. He pulled the last empty chair out and sat down. Ann jumped up and got the First Lieutenant a cup of coffee. Then she sat back in Leo's lap.

"Leo." Bakers said. "Looks like your in pain."

When Ann jumped up a sigh of relief puffed out of Leo. "I'm sorry Babe. It felt so good to have you sitting on my lap." Then he looked at Bakers and quietly added; "Thank youuuuu."

Bakers smiled and quickly looked down to hide it. Ann checked Leo's bandage and his wound was bleeding. Instantly Bakers set one of his men out to get one of the medical team. Ann removed the patch and saw that she had broken one of the stitches. Seconds later one of Bakers' medics gently pushed Ann aside and started pulling things out of his bag. After grabbing a suture he added another stitch to the side of Leo's chest. When they finished Leo went back to bed. The medic gave him something for the pain which made him sleepy.

Ann felt bad about breaking one of Leo's stitches but the others had more important things to talk about. After talking to the others about their attack on the guns and depot Bakers finally left to talk to his men. He asked that no one there go with him and his men when they attacked the guns.

Bakers spent the rest of the day planning the attack and getting his men ready. That night almost all of his men left the woods behind Mike and Britney's home for their mission. Sergeant Myers stayed behind with ten men from his company.

When Bakers and his men left Sergeant Myers came to the house. He pretended to be just visiting but he had orders to make sure that neither Jenifer nor Ann left the house. Bakers did not want them sneaking out and fallowing him and his men.

"Good evening everyone." Myers said as he walked in the back door.

Everyone welcomed him as he walked into the den to check on Leo. They talked for a moment and then Myers got up and walked over to the table. He sat down in a chair and looked at the others at the table who were saying nothing. Then finally Jenifer spoke up.

"Is Bakers gone now?" she asked.

"Yes Ma'am." he replied. "They left a few minutes ago."

Everything in Jenifer and Ann wanted to fallow Bakers but they did not want to mess up his plans. As everyone talked Myers admitted that he was tired and needed to get back to his tent. That was when Jenifer snapped at him.

"You don't need to stay here and watch us." she said.

"What do you mean?" Myers asked with a smile. *How did she know?* he thought to himself.

"Why would Bakers take all of his men except for you and a few others?" Jenifer asked.

"That's just the way he does things." Myers mentioned. "He only took the men he needed for this mission."

Jenifer was upset with her being left out of the mission. The Ghost Warriors had already reconed the depot and the anti-aircraft guns around it. They did the hard things and now some group of American soldiers come in and take over everything. Jenifer was more than just upset. She was downright angry.

The next morning Jenifer woke up early and found David sitting at the kitchen table sipping on a cup of coffee. She poured herself a cup and sat down with him. Suddenly Myers broke in through the back door of the home saying that everyone had to get out of the house. The woods were on fire.

Large drones had dropped incinerator bombs and set the area on fire. With over three hundred American soldiers in the woods the night before one of the large drones spotted all of the heat signatures with its infer red cameras. Lieutenant Colonel Haung decided to burn the large group out and see exactly who they were. It was better than sending in hundreds of soldiers and loosing them in a fight. He figured that they were American soldiers but he was not sure.

By time the sun started coming up everyone was out of the house and running away from the fire with Sergeant Myers and his men in front. Suddenly five black drones seemed to drop right out of the sky and started filming those that were running. They only recorded ten American soldiers but they were still American soldiers. The drones also recorded the members of the Ghost Warriors as well as Mike, Britney, and little Susan.

Mike and Britney carried everything of value out of their home that they could carry. By noon the drones were gone and most of the fire had burned out. Everyone gathered together and went back to the home. Unfortunately; Mike and Britney's home was a total loss.

Britney and Susan held each other crying. Myers and his men walked around the smoking pile of ashes, metal, and still burning wood looking for anything that could be saved. Everything that was left was destroyed. Not having any firearms Mike did manage to save the spear that Leo made for him. Britney saved all of the jerky they had but, little Susan saved the most important thing. She saved her Barbie doll.

"I guess your family will be joining our group now."

Jenifer said to Mike.

"I doubt it." Mike advised. "I have a wife and little girl."

"I see two fighters and a child that can be taught to fight." Jenifer said. "What else are you going to do?"

Mike smiled and stood. After giving Jenifer another big smile he walked over to his wife and daughter. A few minutes later he came back to Jenifer and said; "I guess we will."

"You want to join our group?" Jenifer asked.

"I guess so." Mike said looking puzzled. "My wife and daughter insisted on it."

"We'll have to get you a couple of rifles but … we can do that."

The Ghost Warriors now had six members and a child. Either Britney would have to take care of Susan during all fights giving them five fighters or Susan would have to learn to take care of herself during fights. That would give them six fighters. Then Britney remembered her cousin in Donie. She and her husband had a large lake on their property with plenty of fish in it.

Jenifer talked with Myers about the Ghost Warriors leaving to take little Susan to her aunt's home in Donie. He wanted them to stay there and this did not set well with Jenifer.

"You don't tell me what to do … boy." she told Myers. "We did not fallow Bakers but this has nothing to do with you."

Myers realized that she was actually right. Bakers had ordered him to make sure that the twins did not fallow them and they didn't. On the other hand this was something different. He thought for a moment and then made a decision.

"At least allow me and my men to go with you." Myers mentioned to Jenifer.

"No!" she told him. "If you go you'll want to give orders and I'm the boss of the Ghost Warriors."

Myers thought for a second and then suggested; "You're the boss and I only give orders to my men. I might advise you from time to time but that is all."

Jenifer thought about the Sergeant's offer and then

agreed. She knew that having Myers along with his ten men might complicate things some but as long as he knew that she was in charge she could handle anything else.

Jenifer had one goal for the time being and that was getting little Susan to her aunt's home. Donie was not that far away but it took away from any attacks that the group could be doing. However; Lieutenant Bakers was doing his thing off to the west and they were heading to the north. Until she got the little girl delivered to her aunt she did not want to find any of the enemy.

It took four days to reach the outskirts of Buffalo. Staying far enough to the west of the town to not be seen cost them another day of walking through the brush. Just as they were clear of the town of Buffalo they came upon a squad of North Korean soldiers making rounds around the town. The group lay on the ground but they were still seen.

The nine Korean soldiers surrounded the small group not knowing that Myers and his men were just a short distance away. When Myers saw what was going on he spread his man out to do some capturing, or killing, of their own.

One of the Korean soldiers looked up and saw Lieutenant Myers. Instantly he raised his rifle but, one of Myers' men fired at that soldier killing him with the first shot. Everyone ran for what cover the small trees and brush offered. The fighting went on for over five minutes. When it was over two North Korean soldiers surrendered. The other seven North Korean soldiers were dead. Two of Myers' men were dead and another one was badly wounded.

Myers forced the captured Korean soldiers to dig the graves for the other Korean soldiers and a separate grave a few feet away for the American soldier that was killed. Jenifer handed two of the AK-47s to Mike and Britney along with two extra magazines each.

Then Mike and Britney stripped the dead Korean soldiers of their brown uniforms. They chose soldiers that wore clothing the same size as them. Then they took anything else from the dead Korean soldiers that they needed. By time the

Korean soldiers and the one American soldier was buried everyone was armed and ready to continue.

"Now what should we do with these two?" Myers asked.

"Let me see what I can learn from them first." Leo suggested.

Myers' men tied the two Korean soldiers to trees allowing them to be seated on the ground. Leo began questioning them with Myers asking Leo to translate a few of his questions. Come to find out they were in the process of training some newly arrived soldiers. The North Korean Sergeant was the only seasoned fighter in the group.

The two prisoners were the only survivors of the six new soldiers; straight out of boot camp. As Leo asked questions they were more than pleased to answer them. Unfortunately; they knew nothing. They had just arrived the day before and was being training for working that area. When Myers realized that they really did not know anything worth talking about he thought about what they should do with the two.

"We can't take any prisoners." Jenifer suggested.

"I know. Myers agreed. "I have no problem killing one of these soldiers in a fight but killing any unarmed man bothers me."

Jenifer took in a deep breath and let it out. "Not me." she said as she raised her rifle and fired. After bolting another round in her rifle she fired again killing the second Korean soldier.

With the silencer on her father's 270 rifle the shots were only heard by those there. But the other shots fired during the fight were heard for miles away. With the dead buried the group picked up their things and what they wanted from the dead Korean soldier and left the area.

As they kept to the trees to keep themselves hidden from the drones they were still about two miles from Donie when it started getting dark. They slept in the woods while some of them took turns on watch. During the night they noticed large drones flying over just above the trees. Were they looking for the group? No one got much sleep that night not being sure if one of the drones might drop a bomb on them.

The next morning the group continued to head north to Britney's cousin's home in Donie. Then they came to a large field where an aircraft runway had been built. It was easy to see with the new gravel on the side of the runway that it had just been built. Grass had not yet grown through the gravel. At the northern end of the runway were three large drones. North Korean soldiers were all over the place. Many of them sat in chairs outside one large building. Myers thought that the building had to be their barracks. Jenifer wanted to go around the airfield and deliver Susan to her aunt's home. Then they could recon the airstrip and maybe attack it.

Because they had to travel around the airstrip it was late that night before they came to Britney's cousin's home. Britney knocked on the front door and stepped back. A few seconds later Barbara opened the door. Barbara invited everyone in her home.

"It is so good to see you again." Britney said with a big smile. "We can't stay long but, I need a favor of you."

"Sure." Barbara quickly agreed. "What is it?"

"Mike and I have joined these people ... a small group of resisters." Britney said. "I need you to take care of Susan."

"Of course I will." Barbara agreed.

"What do you mean you will." Britney said. "You have a husband don't you?"

"I did." Barbara said and then she started crying. "Those bastards killed him. He was only planting carrot seeds in front of the house and a patrol walking by just shot him like you would a wild animal. Then they continued walking away laughing." Barbara looked up still crying and added; "They just shot him in the back."

Britney helped her cousin up and gave her a long hug. "I'll make them pay for it." she promised.

The group stayed that night in Barbara's home. It was crowded but they made do. At all times there were at least two of Myers' men on watch during the night. The next morning the group left to recon the airstrip.

Sticking to the trees they found their way to the southern end of the airstrip. Then they moved through the trees and thick brush to the eastern side of the airstrip. There were more trees and brush on that side with two fingers of trees that extended out towards the runway.

Myers set three of his men back to the southern end of the runway. They would fire on any drones trying to take off. Then he took his remaining six men to the northern end of the runway where the barracks and another building were. Jenifer took Mike and Britney to the end of the northern finger of trees while Ann took Leo went to the end of the southern finger of trees. Everyone would open fire after Jenifer did.

When three North Korean soldiers walked out of the barracks Jenifer took aim at one of them and fired. Because of the silencer on her rifle the shot was only heard by Mike and Britney that were with her. When they opened fire everyone else did. In less than three seconds all of the Korean soldiers were dead.

Myers and the six men with him ran into the two buildings. The barracks was empty but the other building was where the pilots flew the drones from. Myers and his men emptied their magazines into the controls for the drones and then ran outside. Not having any explosives they used the AK-47s from the Korean soldiers and shot up the large drones. Two of them caught fire but one was just full of holes. Then suddenly three trucks drove into the airstrip from the southern end.

The three men that Myers sent to the southern end opened fire on the trucks. The trucks stopped and Korean soldiers pilled out. About ten Korean soldiers were in each truck. About ten of them went after the three American soldiers that were firing at them. The remaining twenty Korean soldiers went after Ann and Leo but they had already retreated to the east. Jenifer, Mike, and Britney also retreated back to the large group of trees to the east. After a few minutes of firing at the approaching twenty Koreans Myers and the six men with him also retreated to the east.

When Myers and his six found Jenifer and the others they continued to run to the south. By noon they were about one mile from the airstrip. As they waited they realized that they were no longer being fallowed. After taking count Myers found that he was missing five of his men. All three of them that were at the southern end of the runway had been killed and two with him were also dead. Another one was badly wounded. David was also badly wounded.

The group continued to the south until David collapsed. He could go no father. It was almost dark so Jenifer decided to rest the night there. During the night David and Myers' wounded man died of their wounds. This left Myers with only four men. The Ghost Warriors now had five.

The death of David hit Jenifer hard. She was starting to like him a great deal. She had never allowed herself to get to close to a man before and now that she did, he was dead. She knelt beside David's lifeless body and continued to cry. After a few minutes she stood and walked away.

Myers and his men buried David and their friend there in the woods. Because of all of the tree roots the graves were not as deep as desired but, at least they were buried. The five men that were left at the airstrip would either be buried or burned by the North Koreans.

A few questions bothered Jenifer. Where did the three truck loads of North Korean soldiers come from? How did they know what was going on and get there so fast? Were other large or black drones watching them. If they were are they still up there watching them? Jenifer talked with Myers about these questions and more but he just brushed it off as her being upset over loosing David.

When it was light enough to see, the group left and headed back to Mike and Britney's burned home. That was where Bakers would come when he and his men finished their attacks on the depot and the four anti-aircraft guns. It started raining making the group's walk through the woods even harder. By that night the rain became a storm. No one would get any sleep that night.

When they got to the northern part of the town of Buffalo they had to turn west and go around. They knew when they got to where they had the fight with the Koreans before they got there. The shallow graves had been dug up by wild hogs and other animals and the stench of rotting flesh was very bad. Spending the night there was out of the question so they continued until they could not smell the rotting bodies any more.

The sound of low flying large drones filled the sky all that night. Some in the group were able to sleep but most were not. This meant that most of them had, had no sleep for two nights. Hunger and fatigue was hitting everyone in the group. Large puddles of rain water gave them their needed water saving them from that added problem. Because of the rain it took another three days to get back to Mike and Britney's burned home.

It was around noon when the group crept up to the home. Bakers and his men were not there but most of their tents were. Some of the tents were gone, taken by drifters. Some of the drifters just moved into some of the other tents as if the tents belonged to them. Myers and his men were left there to guard the tents until Bakers got back with his men. This all happened because Myers went with Jenifer and the others. When Bakers did come back Myers would have to explain why some of the tents were gone but, he did not have to explain why and how drifters moved into some of the other tents. They would have to move on.

Myers and his four men went to the people that had moved into the tents and told them that they had to leave. Some of them were armed and none of them wanted to leave. They were all homeless and the tents were their new homes. Myers counted eight families living in twelve tents. Seven of the men in those tents had firearms and Myers really did not want any shooting while children were there.

Myers and his men went back to the tents that the Ghost Warriors had taken closer to the burned down home. After discussing it over with everyone they finally came to a decision.

After that all of the Ghost Warriors along with Myers and his men went back to the drifters.

When Myers walked up to the one man that seemed to be in charge he said; "Here's what we are going to do." Then he noticed some of the armed drifters spreading out. "First of all everyone stop. You're only making this harder."

"The Korean soldiers have burned our homes down and these tents are our new homes." the man in front of Myers said. "We will fight to keep them."

"These tents may be yours to keep." Jenifer said loudly. "But not if one of these fools of yours starts firing."

Myers looked back at Jenifer and said; "Do what?"

"Would you be willing to fight the North Koreans to save your families and these tents as your homes?" Jenifer asked.

The drifters talked it over and agreed. "My name is Jackson. Mark Jackson. What are you offering?"

Jenifer stepped forward and said; "We are the Ghost Warriors and we need more soldiers. If you are willing to fight with us then your families can keep your tents."

Myers looked at Jenifer and asked; "What are you doing?"

"I'm trying to give these people some hope and a reason to fight back. I need soldiers." Jenifer said.

"Could we talk it over during the night and let you know something by morning?"

"If you choose to not join us then be gone by morning." Jenifer ordered.

Jenifer and the others left the drifter's camp and went back to their own camp. As soon as they go there Myers grabbed Jenifer's arm and swung her around.

"What the hell are you doing?" he said low enough that the drifters could not hear.

Jerking her arm out of Myers' hand she yelled; "I am trying to give them some hint of hope and I need soldiers ... if they're willing to fight. What the hell are you doing for them?"

Jenifer left Myers flabbergasted and walked into her tent where she lay down on one of the cots.

"Damn." Myers said still looking at the tent that Jenifer went in. "What the hell was that?"

Ann and Leo walked away laughing while the others were not sure if they should laugh or not. Myers set up guards during the night in case the drifters decided to ambush them while they slept. But that night was a quiet night with an occasional fly over by a few large and black drones. The drifters had campfires but Myers did not warn them. However; for some reason the drones did not bother them all night.

The next morning Myers and his men along with Jenifer and the Ghost Warriors went to the drifter's camp. Jenifer went straight to Mark. After shaking hands she asked him what they had decided to do.

"My family and James and Janet Boyer will join your group." he said. Then he introduced James and Janet to Jenifer. "But this guy over here will not join your group and he will not give up his tent. The others left … as you can see."

"Who are you Sir?" Jenifer asked the man that refused to join or leave.

"None of your damn business." he yelled at Jenifer.

Rog, Rog, Rog." James said as he walked over to the men. "This is Roger … my uncle." he told Jenifer.

Roger quickly raised his rifle and yelled; "Get out'a here and leave me alone."

No one moved so there would be no gun fire. There were six young children in the camp and only Roger did not care.

Suddenly Mark raised his rifle and fired at Roger. Roger fell dead but not before firing a few rounds of his own.

"I didn't like him anyway." Mark said to Jenifer. "He's been in and out of prison at least six times and continued to steal things from family members." Mark suddenly stopped when he looked down at the ground behind Jenifer.

James and Lulu had both been hit in the chest when Roger fired his rifle. They were both dead. They were buried not far from the tents that they called home for a few days. After burying them the others went back to their tents. Mark, Janet, and Brent took down their tent and moved it and their things closer to the others. Mark was armed but not his wife. Brent did pick up Roger's Ruger 10/22 rifle. In his pockets Roger also had over thirty .22 caliber rounds but in his tent he had three quart jars full. The Ghost Warriors now had eight members; seven of which were armed.

The rest of the day was spent catching Mark, Janet, and Brent up on how things were run in the Ghost Warriors. As they talked they burned a great deal of oak wood so that they could make the white paste from the white ashes. The main thing that Jenifer wanted the three of them to know was that she was in charge and Ann was second in charge. As they talked Janet let everyone know that she was not much of a fighter.

"You will be." Jenifer told her. "When bullets start whizzing by your head you'll be surprised at what you'll do."

"It's okay Darlin'." Mark said. "You'll do just fine."

The group continued to talk for hours after it got dark. They made the white paste for Mark, Janet, and Brent and replenished the jars of the others. By midnight everyone was asleep except for Ann and Leo who were standing watch.

Ever since they got back they had been hearing explosions far off to the west. Now the sounds of war were getting closer. Was Bakers and his men being chased by large drones dropping bombs on them? Were the explosions Bakers and his men blowing the guns up? There were so many questions but no answers. One thing was for sure though. The explosions were getting closer.

Throughout the night the explosions got closer and closer to the Ghost Warriors' camp. By morning everyone was already awake and up. When the sounds of war got to within about half a mile from the Ghost warriors it all stopped. For over thirty minutes it actually got quiet. Myers spread his men out so Jenifer did the same.

"Don't shoot anyone wearing an American uniform." Jenifer warned Mike and Brent.

"Yes Ma'am." Brent quickly acknowledged.

For almost an hour nothing moved in front of the group. Then a bush moved; then another and another. Then a voice yelled out.

"Don't shoot. It's us." the voice came from behind the thick brush.

"Who is us?" Brent asked.

"First lieutenant Bakers." he yelled out. "It's just me and a few of my men."

Suddenly Bakers walked out in front of Mark and Brent. He did not know the two so he raised his rifle above his head.

"Is Sergeant Myers here?" Bakers asked.

Lower your rifle Sir." Myers said from a few feet away. "Where is everyone else?"

"Dead or captured." Bakers said. Everything went well until we attacked the second gun. Suddenly they were all around us and what looked like ten black drones were firing those rockets at us. The large drones were dropping bombs on us. We are all that's left. The others were either killed or captured."

Janet tended to the wounded as Jenifer counted Bakers' men. He came in with only seventeen men and three of them were badly wounded. Another nine were wounded but would survive.

After Bakers got some food and water and a little rest they all got together and discussed what all happened. Bakers was a little upset with Sergeant Myers over loosing a few of the tents but now they had more tents than men to go in them. Jenifer told Bakers what they did. Then Myers told him how they came back to some of the tents being gone. Then Bakers told what happed with his attack on the guns.

Chapter 5

The Warehouses

Bakers said that his men spread out and were to hit all four anti-aircraft guns at the same time. Unfortunately; the men that were on their way to the western guns were seen. When the Korean soldiers started firing at them the rest of his men started firing at their targets. Before long there were more North Korean soldiers than Bakers could count. A well organized plan quickly turned into complete chaos and disorder. They never had a chance to attack the depot.

Bakers had no choice but to order a retreat. He said that there had to have been five companies of North Korean soldiers chasing them. He had no idea as to where they came from. He said that judging by how many Korean soldiers were there it looked like they were waiting for him and his men.

"The only thing that I can figure out is that a drone saw our camps ... here ... before we left ... even though we had no campfires." Bakers said. "Haung must have had the Korean soldiers standing by."

"If that is true then why are they not bombing us right now?" Ann asked.

"Good question." Bakers agreed.

The Ghost Warriors and Bakers' men agreed to stay together for a while. Jenifer wanted the added protection while Bakers was looking at having more guns to do what he wanted. However; Jenifer did not like Bakers telling her what to do. The partnership; if that is what it was lasted less than two days.

They still had not moved from Mark and Janet's burned home but Jenifer was already tired of Bakers telling her that they would do some things. Then when he mentioned moving out the next morning to hit the guns again Jenifer refused.

Bakers yelled his orders again and Jenifer raised her rifle in his face. With in seconds all rifles were pointed at someone else.

"Lower your weapons." Myers yelled. "The enemy is out there."

"There you go Sergeant." Bakers said with a smile.

Myers turned so that his rifle was pointed at Bakers. "I was mainly talking to you Lieutenant."

"What are you doing Myers?" Bakers asked

"I guess I'm choosing a side ... Sir." Myers said.

"You'll be court marshaled for this."

"You're a great man to be around Sir but you're an ass out in the field." Myers advised. "I would rather fallow Jenifer than you any day. Now lower your rifles ... everyone."

One by one the rifles started coming down. Bakers and some of his men walked off a little ways. Then he turned and looked at his other men. "You coming or staying here with this looser?"

Bakers' men that did not walk off with Lieutenant Bakers stepped closer to Myers. "I guess they're tired of you too."

Bakers turned again and walked away. Two of the men that were with Bakers at that time changed their minds and walked over to Myers. Myers now had fifteen men with him. Only four went with Bakers.

Bakers and the few men with him packed up their tents and other gear and left the area. They went back to Dallas where he blamed the failure of mission to destroy the anti-aircraft guns on Myers and the fifteen men that took his side. Bakers also put much of the blame on Jenifer and the other Ghost Warriors. He even went as far as saying that Jenifer shot Brandon.

Of course when Dan and Bel-le heard these accusations about their son they went after Bakers. Dan was arrested for threatening First Lieutenant Bakers but only spent one month in jail. Bakers would be found about one month later shot in the head three times. No one heard the shots. Bakers had gone crazy and no one in Dallas liked him. His death was declared as the worst case of suicide ever seen.

Myers and Jenifer agreed that she was the boss if they did anything together but, sometimes he and his men would venture out to have some of their own fun. However; Myers and Jenifer continued to plan all of their attacks together. If they did anything together Jenifer would tell Myers what she needed and he and his men would see that it was done. It worked out perfectly.

Even though Mark and Janet's home had been burn down the newspaper was still delivered to the mailbox. As Mark read the paper out loud for all to hear they all found many reasons to laugh.

On the front page was a large picture of Bakers and his men running for their lives across a large field. Superimposed on the picture were about fifty North Korean soldiers chasing them. It was so easy to see that the picture had been doctored up. The article that covered two full pages told how that the American military tried to attack peace loving American citizens but the North Koreans chased them away. There was no mention of the Americans trying to attack the anti-aircraft guns. On the back page was a small article telling how that the American military also tried to attack the anti-aircraft guns but failed.

The newspaper also had many more of the General's lies in it which Jenifer and Myers knew that many of the American citizens believed. The Liberal Communist could not believe anything good about the Americans even if their lives depended on it.

For almost a week none of them did much except set back and let the wounded heal. Jenifer spent a great deal of time mourning over David's death but Myers was always there to make her feel better. One time she broke down crying and fell into Myers' arms. He held her a good while and let her cry it out.

Jenifer and Myers were not sure what they should do next so, as the wounded men rested Myers sent a few of his men out to get information. Two went to Marquez and two to Jewett. Then he sent three to Centerville for the weekend market.

The two men that Myers sent to Marquez found the bodies of the civilians murdered weeks earlier still laying where they fell. No one was standing around in town and had not since the murders. They did come across a home where a man and his wife stood in the doorway of their home. They walked up to the couple and talked to them for a while. Because of the murdering of American citizens a few weeks earlier no one dared to venture out. The man checked his animal traps at night so he would not be seen. When the two men left they came right back to Myers and gave him their report.

The two men that Myers sent to Jewett came in just as the Mayer was about to have her annual parade. The Mayor of most towns were Chinese appointed North Korean officers placed there for the Chinese to see how they handled things. A mayor could pretty much do what he or she wanted. In Jewett the mayor was a female North Korean Lieutenant Fu.

The two men came into town only after seeing many American citizens walking around. They found many of the civilians there friendly and willing to talk. They walked around and talked to many of the townspeople and learned a great deal.

Lieutenant Fu was a kind woman but also hard on the people if she had to be. She rode the first truck behind the Chinese band. The band played the North Korean National Anthem over and over as if it was the only song they knew. As she passed the two men they saw that she was younger than they figured a First lieutenant would be. She was a pretty woman about thirty years old; maybe younger.

Behind the Mayor was a line of the usual Communist military machinery such as tanks, rocket launchers, and other things. After them came the two companies of North Korean soldiers serving as security in and around Jewett. What came behind them was something that turned the two men's stomachs.

It was a platoon of Americans wearing black uniforms and carrying AK-47s. The last three carried sniper rifles. It was the idea of them being Americans that made both men sick. The front three of them carried a long sign in front of them that read *The New Communist League.*

After the parade the two men walked around town a little and talked to more of the people. When it got dark enough the two men went back and reported to Myers.

The three men that went to Centerville had a bit of a better time. As in Jewett there were hundreds of American citizens walking around. Most of them were setting up makeshift tables or just setting their things on the ground for trade. All kinds of things were there for trade from puppies to food. A few of the older couples had canned boiled meat and vegetables in pint jars. Another old man made toys for the children and a woman had blankets and quilts that they made.

Because it was hard to trade for some things Lieutenant Colonel Haung started a chit program. A chit was a form of money that could be used but only in the Centerville area. If it worked well he would allow it to be used in all of Leon County. The three men got a few of these chits in hopes that they may be able to make their own. They looked easy to copy as no one had any printers and most had no electricity anyway.

Only downtown Centerville had some electricity. The Chinese Command in Austin had many of the electrical plants running including the one a few miles north of Jewett. Only a few of the private citizens had electricity in their homes. These were the elite and richer Liberal Communist traitors that worked with the Chinese and North Koreans. If you wanted electricity you helped the Chinese's Communist invaders.

There were many heavily armed North Korean soldiers walking around. If it were not for all of the Korean soldiers walking around one might think that things were looking better and, maybe they were. Even those that did not work with the Communist government were happy being able to trade their goods.

As the three men got ready to leave Centerville they noticed five trucks coming into town from the west. The trucks were full of young American men and women dressed in what looked like black uniforms. What shocked them was that these

Americans carried rifles. With the sun on its way down it was time to leave Centerville. Three days later the three men reported to Myers.

The three men learned something else and told Myers in their report. They heard that large warehouses were being built northeast of the town of Franklin. They would be located in the middle of large fields giving no cover for anyone trying to attack them from the ground. Large anti-aircraft guns were being installed around them with mine fields around them. If anything the group could attack the convoys delivering the guns, men, and other things needed to build the guns emplacements.

Myers figured that the reason for things being so different in Marquez was because of the attacks on the anti-aircraft guns and depot. The enemy wanted to keep the citizens from moving around in the area of the depot. Jenifer and Myers feared that what happened in Marquez might happen in Franklin. The people had to be warned.

Every now and then the group could hear explosions off to the west. Sometimes American jets would fly over either on their way to a target or on their way back home. From time to time Chinese MIGs would intercept the American jets and a dogfight would start in the skies overhead. In one of these dogfights an American jet was shot down.

The pilot was able to glide his jet into a controlled crash saving his life but, not the life of his navigator. As soon as the jet stopped the pilot got out of his cockpit and ran away from the jet. The jet crashed not far from Marquez so North Korean soldiers were surrounding the downed jet in minutes. When they found the empty seat for the pilot they spread out to find him.

Jenifer and Myers had already left their camp for the town of Franklin. They wanted to warn the civilians there of what happened in Marquez and that it could also happen there. The next day they traveled south of Marquez to avoid any contact with North Korean soldiers. That was when they ran into the pilot of the downed American jet.

Jenifer was leading the group with Myers close behind her. They stepped into a small clearing just as the pilot stepped into the same clearing on the other side. Instantly Jenifer and Myers raised their rifles. The pilot raised his pistol, the only weapon he had.

"Who are you?" Jenifer asked the pilot.

"I'm Lieutenant Bolinski of the Fifth Wing, American Air Force." he said as he lowed his pistol.

Jenifer and Myers lowered their rifles. "I'm Jenifer and this is Sergeant Myers." Jenifer said.

"Sergeant Myers ... with First Lieutenant Bakers?" Bolinski asked.

"Yeah ... that's right." Myers said with a slight smile. "How do you know me?"

"Oh everyone in Dallas knows about you." Bolinski said. "Bakers filed charges on you and your men. Then he went and called the Mountain Ghost and his daughters traitors. That set off a Korean named Wu. A little later Bakers was found dead and no one knows who did it but ... I bet you that Wu fellow did it."

"So what were you attacking?" Jenifer asked.

"And you must be one of the daughters of the Mountain Ghost." Bolinski added not paying attention to Jenifer's question. He stepped over to Ann. "And you must be Ann ... the second daughter of the Mountain Ghost."

"Actually our father was the second Mountain Ghost." Ann advised.

"Oh yeah ... he was." Bolinski said. "I'm sorry to hear about your parents. I met your father one time but only for a few seconds. He shook, my hand."

"Why was he shaking your hand?" Jenifer asked.

"He shook all of our hands ... graduation from flight school." Bolinski said as he smiled.

"I guess you now a part of our group now." Jenifer said.

"What group?" Bolinski asked.

"We're the Ghost Warriors." Myers quickly said. "Now your one of us."

"Sounds good to me but I need something other than just this 38 caliber revolver. I only have six rounds in it."

"We'll find you something soon." Myers assured him. "You don't mind an AK-47 do you?"

"Not at all." Bolinski said with a big smile. "I prefer it over the M-16 anyway."

"Why is that?" Brent asked.

The AK can be thrown in the mud and it will still fire but you get an M-16 muddy and it stops working." he advised the young man. "The AK rounds are a little larger than the .223 also. As far as I'm concerned it is an all around better weapon."

After explaining what they were doing Jenifer reminded Bolinski of their chain of command. She was in charge with Ann second in charge. If they needed a third in charge Myers would be it. This shocked Myers because no one had told him that he was third in charge.

"I know you're a lieutenant but until we get to know you your rank is someplace below Sergeant Myers." Jenifer reminded him. "We know the Sergeant and we just met you."

"He probably knows more about surviving than I do anyway." Bolinski said. "I have no problem with that."

The group continued on their way to Franklin. All they knew about the warehouses being built there was that they would be northeast of the town. They knew nothing about where the anti-aircraft guns would be. As they stayed a few hundred yards south of Highway 79 they saw many military convoys taking equipment and building supplies towards Franklin. It was easy to see that the Chinese were going all out on this project.

Crossing the Navasota River was easy. The water level was down. The two bridges over the river and a low area had North Korean soldiers guarding them. They had to cross the river farther downstream.

With the warehouses being built on the western side of Highway 79 the group crossed the highway about three miles from Franklin. This might have kept them from getting to close to the warehouse construction site but they still had no idea as to where the anti-aircraft guns were going to be built. They had to be careful with every step they took.

Bolinski told Jenifer and Myers that he flew over the town of Franklin many times and reminded them that it was surrounded by large fields and hardly no trees at all. They had just crossed the highway when they came upon the construction of an anti-aircraft gun. Stopping in a small group of trees they watch for a while.

Bolinski was right. As far as they could see the only trees large enough to hide the group were where the guns were being built. They would have to plan something different if they were going to attack these guns. While the Ghost Warriors stayed and watched the gun's construction Myers sent five of his men to the south fallowing the highway to see what was down that way. Then he took his other men to the north and crossed the highway to see what was around there. Jenifer sent Ann and most of the others back to a spot just south of Marquez where they would wait for everyone to group up. She had Mike stay with her while his wife went with the others.

The five men that Myers sent to the south came upon another anti-aircraft gun construction that evening. As they watched through the night they noticed that the work was being done by Americans being used as slave labor. They also noticed that not one but three guns emplacements were being built there. The next morning they left and went back to the designated area just south of Marquez.

Myers and the men with him took two days to find the northern anti-aircraft guns. Like with the others three of these guns were being set up with minefields around them. Then he sent five of his men to the north to circle around to find any western guns if there were any.

After spending one day watching the construction of the northern guns they left that night. Just after crossing Highway 79 they went to where Jenifer and Mike were watching the eastern guns but, they were not there. From there they went to the designated area south of Marquez.

When Myers and the men with him got back to Jenifer and the others they waited for the others that he sent to checkout the western guns. After one week they still had not returned.

On the seventh night Jenifer sent Ann and Leo into town to take a look. They were not to even get close to any North Korean soldiers. When it was dark they left for town.

As Ann and Leo took their time walking into town they saw others gathering at a home across the railroad tracks from the gas station where so many had been murdered. When Ann and Leo walked up to the others they stopped talking.

"Who are you two?" one of the old women asked.

"I'm Ann and this is my boyfriend Leo." Ann said. "We're new in the area."

"Well then don't cross the tracks." the old woman said. "Death waits for you over there."

The woman told Ann and Leo what happened at the gas station on the other side of the tracks. They pretended not to know and continued to talk to the small group. Before long those there were friendly to them and even laughing a few times. Then suddenly everyone stopped talking and went into the home. As Ann and Leo looked up they saw another convoy driving through town on their way to the gun emplacements.

"What's that?" Leo asked the man standing inside behind the almost closed door.

"You don't know … Comrade." the man said.

"He is a North Korean that deserted and is now with me." Ann said to the man.

"It's a North Korean convoy taking supplies to the warehouses being built just south of here.

Ann and Leo continued to play dumb as the others talked more than they should have. Around midnight the others turned in leaving Ann and Leo by themselves. They took it as a hint and left. As they walked back to Jenifer and the others they saw a platoon of North Korean soldiers walking down the road towards them. They quickly hit the trees and brush on the side of the road before they were seen.

As the soldiers passed Ann and Leo held hands. For a few

seconds the North Korean Sergeant stopped his men. Ann and Leo thought that maybe they had been seen. But the Sergeant walked around his men yelling something in Korean and then ordered them to continue marching. Before leaving the brush they kissed and then stood and left for Jenifer and the others.

When the North Korean soldiers were far gone Ann and Leo continued on their way back to Jenifer and the others. Being careful they stopped every now and then to look around but finally made their way back to the others.

When Ann and Leo got back they found out that the five men that Myers had sent to checkout any western guns still had not come back. The Ghost Warriors and Myers' men discussed what could have happened but they could not send anyone to find out. The five men were probably captured or killed and anyone trying to find them might also get captured or killed. They finally decided to wait another three days.

The Ghost Warriors did not know it but the North Koreans had cleared out most of the buildings on the north eastern side of Franklin. Everyone living in the area was warned not to go into these buildings. A barbed wire fence was put up down the street blocking off these buildings from the civilians living in Franklin.

After waiting three days for the five missing men the Ghost Warriors and, Myers and his men decided to proceed with their previous plans. They would go to warn the people of Franklin that what happened in Marquez could happen there.

A heavy rain hit that day making it hard to do any traveling. They stayed east of Highway 79 giving them more woods to travel through than the western side did. It took four days to reach the Navasota River which was now swollen with the rainfall which was still coming down. There was no way that they were going to cross their usual spot. When the river was down they simply crossed a shallow area but now that shallow area was over fifteen feet deep. They would have to go back up to Highway 79 and see if the Korean soldiers were still guarding the bridge.

Because of the muddy conditions it took the rest of the day

to get to the highway. Myers slowly stepped up on the side of the highway and looked both ways. It was all clear except for a few lights and movement around the bridge. After going back to let Jenifer know what he saw he left with two men. They worked their way up the side of the highway until they could see how many soldiers there were.

A North Korean platoon had set up on both sides of the bridge with a sandbag wall and a large gun behind the walls. Fifteen soldiers were at each end of the first bridge and all walking traffic had been topped. Usually a few American civilians could be seen at almost anytime going one place or another but there was no one except the soldiers at the bridge. Crossing the bridge was completely out of the question.

Myers and the two men with him went back to tell Jenifer what they found. They could wait a week or so for the river to go down or abort the mission completely. There was one more course of action. There were eighteen of them so, with the element of surprise they might be able to rush the bridge. Being outnumbered almost two to one many if not all of them would be killed. Rushing the bridge was quickly dismissed.

The rain finally stopped so they decided to go deeper into the woods far from the highway and wait. As Jenifer took the first watch for the night she took time to ask help from God.

"We need some help here Father. We can't cross the river and we need to warn the people of Franklin." Jenifer stopped praying for a moment as she thought. *"We're also running low on food too Lord. Got plenty of water but not much food and we cannot hunt or the soldiers on the bridge will hear the shot and check it out. Father ... we need your help."*

Jenifer looked up at the clouds. Every now and then the clouds would break to show a star or two. At midnight Myers relieved her and she went back to camp where she fell right to sleep.

The next morning Ann woke Jenifer up. "Hurry up." she urged her sister. "You've gota see this."

Jenifer got up and staggered behind Ann. She was still wiping her eyes when Ann stopped. Jenifer looked up and in the dim daylight she could see that the river was low.

"That's impossible." Jenifer insisted. "It's ... impossible."

"Maybe so but we need to cross while we can." Myers suggested.

"Get everyone across." Jenifer told Ann. Then she looked at Myers and said; "I need you and your men on the other side scouting the area out."

"You got it." he acknowledged.

Myers and his men quickly crossed to the other side and looked around. Within a few minutes the others went back to the camp, got their things, and crossed the river. Once the Ghost Warriors were on the other side of the river Jenifer had them settle down and wait for Myers and his men.

Suddenly there was gunfire a short distance to the west of everyone. Jenifer figured that Myers and his men were in trouble so she ordered the Ghost Warriors to fallow her. As the other Ghost Warriors fallowed behind Jenifer she came to a small clearing. On the other side were three North Korean soldiers firing to her left. Unable to see who or what they were shooting at she raised her 270 rifle and took aim. Leo stepped up beside her and aimed his AK-47. Jenifer took down one of the soldiers and Leo got the other two. Instantly she ordered everyone to fallow her.

As Jenifer crossed the clearing she saw Myers and his men to her left. The soldiers had been shooting at them. The Ghost Warriors and Myers and his men ran for their lives. After about one hundred yards they stopped. The mud was making it hard to get anyplace.

As everyone lay in the mud they heard North Koreans talking in the clearing that they had just crossed. After a few minutes the soldiers went back to the bridge carrying their three friends.

Once again the Ghost Warriors were saved by a prayer. The lake was very low so when the rain hit those operating the dam gates closed them. This raised the water leveling the lake

but dropped the level of the river.

Chapter 6

The River

One of Myers' men had been wounded when the three North Korean soldiers attacked them back at the river. The bullet passed through his right thigh so, two others had to help him walk. By the evening of the second day he was able to walk on his own but they all had to move slower than normal. Because of this it took almost a week to reach the southern outskirts of Franklin.

For over a mile to the north, east, and south of Franklin the area was covered with large open fields. There were very few clusters of trees to hide in. The only place to hide was in the town itself. With this in mind the group moved into one small group of trees just southeast of Franklin and waited until dark.

Jenifer and Myers discussed how they were to go about warning the civilians about what might and could happen to them. The Ghost Warriors would do the informing of the civilians while Myers and four of his men would recon the warehouse construction more. The wounded man would stay in the trees and rest while the other four would go with the Ghost Warriors to help Jenifer in any way needed.

When it got dark Myers and his four men moved through town towards the warehouse construction site. Moving from building to building and trying not to be seen by anyone they had only made it to Highway 79 by 0200 hours. By time the sun started to turn the eastern sky blue they had come to the barbed wire fence but, they had to find a place to hide. Myers had his men move into a vacant building close to the fence so they could watch during the day to see what was happening. They had not heard about the fencing off of part of the town.

Jenifer split her group into four teams of two with one of

Myers' men with each couple. The four teams would spread out so that they could cover more homes at one time.

By the time it started to get daylight the Ghost Warriors had already covered part of southern Franklin. Most of the civilians would not open their doors until they heard English speaking voices. Even then the many of the civilians would not open their door to someone that could be trying to invade their home.

Myers was farther north of the Ghost Warriors when Jenifer came upon a North Korean patrol. They quickly hid but with the sun coming up they really needed to find a place to hide during the day. Jenifer waved to the other three teams and they went into an old mechanic shop garage.

The side door to the garage was open making it easy to get in but the door was jammed open and would not shut. If anyone came by they would be able to see the group in there so Jenifer had everyone pile things in the door opening. A few old tires were put in the doorway at first but that was not enough. By time it was light enough to see the doorway was so jammed with trash that no one would try to get inside.

The group stayed quiet all day not wanting to draw any attention to the garage. During the day it was very active outside but no one tried to get into the garage itself. Although they were behind a barricaded door Jenifer still had someone stand watch while everyone else slept.

Around noon a North Korean patrol stopped just outside the garage to rest in the shade of the building. They took time to eat. When they finished they joked around with each other. The Sergeant of the patrol got up and walked around the garage. When he came to the door he stopped. Leo was on watch at this time and watched the Sergeant behind the pile of trash in the doorway. The Sergeant tried to move a few of the things blocking the doorway but quickly gave up and went back to his man. After ordering them to get back into formation they marched off in a manner that only a hard core North Korean soldier could do. With each step they would swing their arms like they were trying to clear out everything on both sides of them.

One of Myers' men, Corporal Tads stepped close to the doorway and looked through a crack in the tin siding. His heart was beating ninety to nothing. He listened for any sound that might hint that someone was still outside when Jenifer stepped up beside him and put her hand on his shoulder. Tads jumped accidentally knocking an empty paint can off of the shelf.

The Korean Sergeant stopped his soldiers and looked back at the garage. Then he ordered his men to stand fast while he check the garage out again. As he walked away he ordered the last two men in his formation to fallow him. Ordering the rest of his men to at-ease they turned to watch.

When the North Korean Sergeant got to the garage he send the two soldiers around to the left and right side of the building.

"Nada." he waited a few seconds and repeated; "Nada."

One of the soldiers with him spoke English and yelled; "Come out. The Sergeant wants you to come our."

By this time everyone in the garage was wide awake and ready to fight. With so much piled in the doorway there was no way to get out quickly and they thought that they were surrounded. Finally Jenifer agreed to surrender. As the soldiers pulled the things away from the doorway enough that she could go outside then she would pretend to surrender. Once she was outside the others could run outside and attack the soldiers.

Jenifer called out to the Sergeant; "I'm alone."

The Sergeant called the rest of his men to help. As they surrounded the garage two of them started removing the junk in the doorway. Tads stood by the door ready to throw Jenifer her rifle. When the doorway was cleared enough Jenifer stepped outside. Suddenly Tads fired a shot hitting the Korean soldier coming in the garage. Then he threw Jenifer her rifle. At this point a sniper's rifle was not what she needed. In seconds though the others were outside firing their rifles and in less than fifteen seconds all of the Korean soldiers were dead.

Jenifer picked up an AK-47 and tossed it to Lieutenant Bolinski.

"Now you have a rifle." she told him. Then she yelled at the others saying; "Strip'm clean."

In less than a minute the group was on their way more armed than before. Not only did they collect twenty five full AK magazines but each soldier also carried grenades. Anyone that did not have a canteen did now. Before leaving, the group smashed all of the AK-47s that they did not take. Bolinski traded his shinny blue flight jacket for a brown North Korean jacket. All of the Korean pistols and holsters were also taken by the group.

It was still daylight so the group had to quickly find another place to hide. An old man in a house down the street had seen what happened and called for the group to come to him. As they ran to him he opened his back door and let them all in. Then he saw Leo in his North Korean uniform and froze not sure what he should do. Behind him was Ann and a couple of the others so he allowed Leo to come in as well.

When they were all in the house the old man shut and locked the door. Then he turned with a pistol in his hand. "Is he one of you?" he asked as he pointed the pistol at Leo.

Ann quickly stepped in front of Leo and said; "He's been one of us for a while now."

The old man took in a deep breath and lowered the pistol. "I'm sorry ... young man but your people ... I hate you all but you ... I might be able to like ... maybe."

"He's a very likable fellow Sir." Ann tried to assure him.

"Yeah!" he said as he looked close at Leo. "He does look like he is."

Jenifer warned the old man about what happened in Marquez and that it could happen in Franklin and then told him that they were warning everyone. Then she told him that they needed their rest because they warned people at night when they could move around.

The old man got out a few cots and blankets and before long most of the group was fast asleep. Jenifer and Tads stayed up to watch the place in case someone saw them coming into the old man's home. Finally Jenifer fell asleep. Around three in the evening Tads woke up.

Soon after the group found refuge in the old man's home the streets were full of North Korean soldiers. The dead soldiers were loaded into trucks and carried away. By time it was dark there were still to many Korean soldiers on the streets so the group would have to wait. It would be to risky to try to go outside.

Myers and his men used the darkness to cross the barbed wire and go into the secured area. They found a three story building two blocks from the edge of town and checked it out. From the third floor they could watch everything going on in the warehouse construction area.

The warehouse construction site was all lit up with lights. American citizens were being used as slave labor and the construction continued all day and night. Two shifts were used working the prisoners twelve hours a day or night and seven days a week. Myers wanted to get a closer look but he did not dare get any closer.

The streets inside the secured area were patrolled by three squads during the day and two squads during the night. *I would have doubled the patrols at night.* Myers thought to himself. *Who ever is in charge is not all that smart.*

For three days and nights Myers and his four men watched the construction site. On the evening when they were to move out someone saw one of Myers' men in the window. A company of North Korean soldiers surrounded the building. A shot was fired from a Korean soldier and the fight was on.

Two of Myers' men covered the stares while Myers and the other two men took a window to fight from. One of the men watching the stares was shot and then an explosion went off taking the other one out. Myers ran to the stares and shot three Korean soldiers trying to come up. From two blocks away a Chinese tank fired and the side of the building blew away killing the other two men. Myers now stood alone.

Myers fired two rounds at Korean soldiers trying to come

up the stares. He was out of ammo. More Korean soldiers came up to the floor where Myers was and stood in front of him.

"Geugeo tteol-eo tteulyeo. Geugeo tteol-eo tteulyeo." one of the Korean soldiers yelled as he waved his AK-47 at the floor.

Myers knew that he had no chance and dropped his rifle. He could have pulled his pistol to continue fighting but the soldiers would have cut him down before he even got his pistol out of the holster. Two of the soldiers grabbed Myers and walked him down stares to the outside of the building.

Myers was taken to the construction site where he was thrown into a small building. The door was locked and a guard was placed outside. The building had only two windows but they had been replaces with center blocks with the holes facing out to give some light inside. The holes were way to small to escape through. As Myers looked around he found the building was empty. There was nothing that could be used to help in an escape. Then he noticed the center block walls. The building had recently been built for the purpose of holding prisoners.

The next morning the door opened and a bowl of gummy rice was laid on the floor. When the door closed Myers went to look at the bowl. When he picked up the bowl he found the rice so gummy that he picked it up from the bowl with his hand. It was very sticky and cold but, it was food. After setting the bowl back on the floor by the door he went back to the far corner and sat on the floor where he enjoyed this fine meal that was given to him.

By this time Jenifer and the others were still inside the old man's home. As she looked outside she noticed that Korean soldiers were going from home to home and searching them. She had everyone get ready for another fight.

"Father ... please help us. If they come here we'll be trapped. Please help us Father?"

The group set up behind furniture and counters in the kitchen; anything that gave them some kind of cover. Jenifer looked outside through a thin cloth that the old man had placed over the window for privacy. She saw a few Korean soldiers walk up to the front door. She got ready for another fight. Just as the soldier in front was about to knock on the door another Korean soldier across the road yelled at him. The soldiers at the old man's door walked over and talked with the soldier across the road. Then the soldiers went to the next home and continued their search.

Jenifer sighed in relief. "I guess he forgot what home he was searching and skipped this one." she advised the others.

The group spent the rest of the day in the old man's home. Jenifer and Tads talked about continuing with their mission but it was becoming more dangerous by the day. There were just to many Korean soldiers walking around. They decided that if they could leave that night they would head out of the area.

When it got dark Jenifer looked outside. For over an hour she and others looked for any sign of Korean soldiers but they saw no one. Finally around midnight she thanked the old man for his help and stepped outside. Then she took a few steps away from the door and the others came out as well. Within a minute the old man was looking down an empty street.

The group headed south using the buildings for cover. By morning they had worked their way out of the town and back into the group of trees just southeast of Franklin. They found the wounded man that they left but he was dead. He had been shot in the head. A patrol must have found him. Tads and his men took turns on watch while they all waited for the dark of the next night. Then they would leave the area.

Myers and his men were suppose to have been in the group of trees by this time but they had not shown up. That night Jenifer sent everyone except Tads and one of his men back to the gathering point south of Marquez. They would wait there until Jenifer, Tads, and the other man got there.

Ann lead the group away from the group of trees and to the river. Unfortunately; the river was up again so they had to wait until it went down. Ann took the group farther away from the bridge so that they would not be heard or found by any

North Korean patrols.

While Jenifer, Tads and the other man waited a North Korean patrol came close to them. Fearing that they might be spotted the other man jumped out and started firing. As the Korean soldiers returned fire Jenifer and Tads crawled under some dead tree limbs and leaves. The shooting stopped and the Korean patrol searched the trees for more people. After a few minutes they left. At one time one of the Korean soldier stepped on Jenifer's hand under the leaves. For what seemed to be minutes the soldier just stood there but, Jenifer did not move.

When it was quiet for a while Jenifer and Tads crawled out from under the branches and leaves. Jenifer held her hand but she knew that she would be okay. Luckily the Korean soldier did not weigh much. Jenifer and Tads waited until the next night before giving up on Myers and leaving the trees.

Rain came again and this time it was a storm. Although it only rained a couple of hours it came down hard dumping a great deal of water on the area. The area around the river became even more flooded. Jenifer and Tads had to wait on higher ground until the water went down. Only then would they be able to find the others.

Because of the flooding Ann had to move the others farther back towards Franklin where there was higher ground. Ann and Jenifer were only a quarter of a mile apart but neither of them knew it.

Both groups hunkered down staying quiet and still. Any sound or movement could send North Koran soldiers down on them. Ann and her group were farther downstream from the Highway 79 bridge than Jenifer and Tads were.

Knowing that they were close to the bridge Jenifer and Tads spread out some in case one of them were spotted by a Korean patrol. They were close enough that they could hear the Korean soldiers on the bridge talking from time to time. Then suddenly Tads saw movement. Someone was coming from the area of the bridge. He waved to Jenifer and then pointed towards the movement. Then he took aim and waited.

As Tads watched the bushes moving in front of him Jenifer saw the bushes to her right move. Without warning she felt the cold steal of a rifle barrel against her neck.

"Geugeo tteol-eo tteulyeo." a North Korean soldier behind her yelled. Then with his rifle pushing a little harder against her neck he repeated his demand. "Geugeo tteol-eo tteulyeo."

Tads heard the Korean soldier yelling and looked over at Jenifer. He took careful aim and fired. Then both he and Jenifer started firing but with Jenifer armed with a bolt action rifle they decided to run in the opposite direction.

"Run for it." Tads insisted.

Jenifer had no problem with him screaming orders at that point. They did not know it but they were both running directly towards Ann and the others. When Ann heard the shots being fired she had everyone spread out. She warned everyone that the North Korean soldiers could be firing at Jenifer and Tads so be careful. However; Brent must not heard her. As soon as he saw bushes moving he fired.

"Hold your fire." Jenifer yelled as she saw Brent. Ann continued to run until she got past them. Seconds later a line of North Korean soldiers came through the bushes and everyone opened fire. The firefight lasted only five minutes. Any Korean soldiers that survived the fight headed back to the bridge. Jenifer knew that they would be coming back with reinforcements so she had everyone fallow her. Then she realized that Tads was not there.

"Find Tads." Jenifer ordered. "Hurry. We don't have long."

Mike was the one that found Corporal Tads. Tads had been shot but he was still alive. Mike and Leo helped Tads up and walked him to Jenifer. She quickly looked him over and saw that he had been hit in the left cheek. The bullet came in from in front of him and exited below his ear. He was bleeding but not so bad that he could not be moved.

With the river to the east and the bridge to the north Jenifer had everyone head back towards Franklin. When they came to a road that someone had made through the woods they took it to the south. Ann, Leo, and Bolinski stayed behind to watch for anyone fallowing them. If Korean soldiers did show up the three would head towards Franklin in hopes of leading them away from the others.

After the group was about one mile from the bridge they stopped. Tads could walk no farther. Although he was not bleeding bad he had still lost a great deal of blood because his wound had not been tended to. When they stopped Jenifer got right to taking care of Tads' face.

Ann, Leo, and Bolinski waited until dark before trying to find the others. They did not know how far Jenifer took the others so they finally stopped to wait until morning. Ann had Leo and Bolinski spread out to cover a larger area. They were very tired anyway.

The rain came back that night. It came down hard for many hours washing away any tracks they had made in the mud. Jenifer worried about her sister not showing up during the night but there had been no gunfire so she had to be safe. Then she realized that with the cloud cover there was no moonlight to see by.

Tads needed a great deal of rest so Jenifer planned on staying there for a while. They could not cross the river and Franklin was no longer a friendly place. Being about one mile south of the bridge was perfect. No self respecting North Korean city boy would go so far from the highway and so deep into the woods.

Jenifer set out guards to stand watch throughout the night. They went a little ways towards the bridge and hid. The rain continued through the night although it did slow some. By morning the rain had become a light sprinkle. By noon the next day the rain stopped and the clouds cleared.

Ann, Leo, and Bolinski had still not shown up so Jenifer sent out a few people to go up as far as the bridge and then come back. The ones that went to look for Ann, Leo, and Bolinski came back in about four hours. When they heard Korean voices they turned and came back. They were close enough to the bridge to find the three but, thanks to the rain there were no signs of them.

"Sorry Jenifer." one of the three said. "We saw nothing."

"Maybe they were ... captured." Jenifer barely said.

The others tried to convince her that her sister was okay but she knew better. Ann, Leo and Bolinski were accomplished fighters but there was no gunfire. *Could they have been captured without firing a shot*? Other questions bothered Jenifer but she was convinced that the three were captured.

When Ann, Leo, and Bolinski had gone just over a half a mile from the bridge they could not believe that the others would have gone farther. That was when they turned towards Franklin. They had not been captured at all but, with the added rain the river was swelling even more.

Because of the rising river both groups had to move farther to the west; closer to Franklin. With them being so far from any activity they moved during the day. When Jenifer's group stopped she looked at Tads again.

"You were shot from the front as you were running in." she told him. "You know who shot you?"

"Yeah!" he said but it hurt to talk so he pointed.

When Jenifer looked at who Tads was pointing at she saw Brent sitting on an old log. He looked sad probably because he knew what he did but was to scared to admit it.

"Accident." Tads was barely able to say making sure that Jenifer knew that Brent did not mean to shoot him.

Jenifer stood and walked over to Brent and had a quiet talk with him. In seconds he was crying. Mark and Janet walked over to their son. Jenifer explained to them that Brent had accidentally shot Tads but, Tads was not angry. Then she walked away and back to Tads.

"This river is going to keep us here for a while you know." Tads told Jenifer. "Maybe I can't do much but the rest of you really should."

"What do you have in mind?" Jenifer asked.

"We are the Ghost Warriors right?"

"Yes." Jenifer replied.

"Then when are these ... ghost ... going to start terrorizing the enemy again?"

Jenifer walked away and into the woods. As she disappeared into the darkness of the brush she sought guidance from a much higher source.

"What should I do now Father? Tads is right. We need to start ... the Ghost Warriors need to start doing things. What should we do Father?"

Jenifer sat on a log just out of camp and looked up into the sky. She waited for God to give her an idea. Finally a plan began to form in her head. She stood and walked back into camp. As she stood there she looked around. Seeing that Brent was feeling bad she gave him something to do.

"Brent." she said. "I need you to build a fire."

"That will give off smoke and it could bring them down on us." Mark insisted.

"It will also give us white ashes and the white paste we will be needing from now on."

Mark knew what Jenifer was thinking and smiled. Then he helped Brent with the fire. Within two hours there was enough ashes for all of the Ghost Warriors.

"For all of you new members of the Ghost Warriors ..." Jenifer said out loud. We are the Ghost Warriors and it's about time we started looking like ghosts. We are about to start putting terror back into the minds of the enemy."

The others started to cheer but Jenifer warned them about not being loud. Not being able to show how they felt through loud cheering they actually jumped for joy and started hugging each other.

Now what are we going to do? Jenifer asked herself.

Jenifer called on Mark and Janet to go scout out the bridge. She needed to know how many North Korean soldiers were on this side of the river. Mark and Janet got their rifles and gear and left for the bridge. Now it was a matter of waiting for them to come back.

About an hour after it was light enough to see Mark and

Janet came back to the camp. They reported that there were ten Korean soldiers at each end of the bridge. They took twelve hour shifts with five of them in each shift. This meant that if attacked then half of them would be asleep. This was the weakness that Jenifer was looking for.

As the Ghost Warriors walked through the woods to the bridge Jenifer stopped them all. There was movement in the bushes ahead. As they waited Mark saw Ann and Leo walking towards them. He called out to them and they stopped. After realizing that the others were coming towards them they continued. As they got closer Jenifer could see that Ann and Leo were helping Bolinski walk. He had been shot.

"You three get back to the camp." she told Ann. Then she ordered Brent to show them where the camp was.

By that evening Jenifer had the Ghost Warriors close enough to the bridge to see the Korean soldiers standing guard. All of the Ghost Warriors were painted up with the white paste and their cloths were even torn so that they looked like the dead. She spread them out so that they could fire on the soldiers. Then she took aim at one of the soldiers with her father's 270 rifle and fired.

Instantly the Ghost Warriors opened fire on the North Korean soldiers at the southern end of the bridge. Within a couple of minutes all of the Korean soldiers were dead and not one Ghost Warrior had been hit. Jenifer ordered her warriors to spread out on both sides of the highway. She knew that the Korean soldiers at the other end of the bridge would come to help their friends.

In less than a minute after the battle at the southern end of the bridge was over two trucks with fifteen North Korean soldiers stopped about two hundred yards from the southern end of the bridge. As the soldiers pilled out of the truck the Ghost Warriors cut them down. This battle did not last a minute.

Jenifer ordered some of the Ghost Warriors to get into the back of the truck. It would drive slowly towards the northern end of the bridge with the others walking behind it. Jenifer had some of the Ghost Warriors walk so that they could run into the trees as soon as they crossed the first bridge.

What was called the Navasota River Bridge was actually two bridges. The southern most bridge actually crossed a low area that flooded after most rains and the northern bridge crossed the Navasota River itself.

The North Korean soldiers at the northern end of the bridge did not fire on the truck until it got to the southern end of the river bridge. Jenifer ordered Mike to keep low to the floorboard and continue to slowly drive the truck towards the Korean soldiers. By time the truck got to the northern end of the bridge only three Korean soldiers remained. They quickly surrendered but Jenifer ordered them to be shot anyway.

Jenifer sent Mark back to the camp to get his son Brent and, Ann, Leo, and Bolinski. He had to hurry as time was not on their side. Mark took the truck so that he could get to the other end of the southern bridges quicker. It was almost a half mile trip not including a good half mile walk to the camp.

While Mark was gone the others stripped the Korean soldiers of everything that they could use. However; it did not take long for Korean reinforcements to get there but, Jenifer was ready.

As the two trucks of North Korean reinforcements pulled up to the northern bridge the Ghost Warriors opened fire. By time Mark and the others got back to the others the fight was over but, Jenifer knew that other Korean soldiers would be on their way. *Hurry up Mark.* She thought to herself.

As soon as the truck got back to the others they headed into the woods to the east. Seconds later two platoons of North Korean soldiers rolled in. As soon as the trucks stopped the soldiers pilled out and stood in formation. Then some Chinese officer sent them all into the woods; one platoon on one side and the other platoon on the other side.

Chapter 7

Myers

As the Ghost Warriors fought through the mud to the east Myers was having his own problems. When he was captured he was thrown into a room that looked like it had been quickly constructed for holding prisoners. He spent three days there only being fed once a day and it was just a bowl of yellow rice. When the Korean guards brought the rice to him they laughed. He knew that they had urinated on his rice thinking that it was funny.

When the guard came back for the bowl Myers threw the rice on him. The guard and two other Korean soldiers came in and beat Myers until he passed out. Myers woke up the next day around noon with another bowl of rice sitting by the door. This time the rice was white.

He picked up the bowl and smelt the rice. It did not have any unusual odors to it so he tasted it. Tasting only rice he sat down in a corner of the room and ate it. When he finished he tossed the bowl over by the door.

The guard outside must have heard the bowl hit the door as he opened it and picked the bowl up. He gave Myers a look and then closed the door. Myers heard a padlock click shut securing the door.

The North Korean guard had an empty look on his face that bothered Myers. The guard did not smile, frown, or anything else. He showed no emotion at all. He just looked deep into Myers' eyes and then shut the door.

Myers sat back in his corner and looked around. There were no windows but one wall had cinderblocks turned on their sides that gave Myers a place to look outside but, the holes were to small to escape through.

That evening Myers heard the padlock on the door being

unlocked. The door opened and in stepped two armed North Korean soldiers. Then a well dressed officer stepped in behind them.

"I am Captain Choe ... Head of Security in and around this facility." the officer said. "Now ... who are you?" Choe asked as he patted his hand with a small whip.

Myers just looked at him and smiled so Choe stepped closer and asked his name again. Still not getting an answer Choe quickly slapped the whip against Myers' face. Myers quickly turned his head away as the whip stung bad. A few second later he turned his head back to Choe.

"You do know your name right?" Choe asked. Again there was no answer from Myers so Choe used the whip again.

The side of Myers' face was starting to bleed as the whip cut into his cheek. "My name is Myers ... Sergeant Myers of the United States military."

"In case you have not heard ... there is no United States." Choe said with a smile.

"Oh there's more of us than there are of you foul smelling bastards." Myers said also smiling.

"Well ... Sergeant Myers ... you are going to help in building my warehouses. Choe advised Myers. "You have fun now."

Choe gave orders to the two soldiers and then left. The two soldiers grabbed Myers by the arms and lead him down a dirt road to a long building. The guard at that door unlocked the door and opened it. Myers was pushed inside the building and the door closed behind him.

Myers stood in the darkness of the building and tried to look around. It was to dark to see anything. Suddenly he heard movement and then a voice. "Don't worry man. No one here is going to hurt you."

A match to his left flashed as the man holding it lit a candle. With the little light that there was Myers was able to see that bunk beds lined both sides of the building. As the candle got closer Myers could see that many American men were also there.

"You have no reason to fear us." the man with the candle said. "My name is Rand; Rand Wilson and you are now one of us."

"What do you mean one of us?" Myers asked.

"You'll be working here until we finish the warehouses or you die." Rand advised.

Rand showed Myers a few of the empty bunks and told him to choose one. Then Rand and the others went back to their bunks leaving Myers to stand there all by himself.

Using his hand Myers wiped the sand and dirt off of what used to be called a soft bed and lay down. Others were talking so Myers listened so he could learn to what all was going on. Before long it got quiet and only Myers was still awake. To his surprise he fell asleep soon after that.

Before it was even daylight enough to see lights turned on a metal trashcan was thrown down the walkway between the bunk beds. Myers saw that the other men flew out of their beds as quickly as they could and stood beside them so he did the same.

A Chinese lieutenant slowly walked down the walkway just inches from the prisoners but no one tried to jump him. Myers was wondering about this when the Lieutenant stopped in front of him.

"You're ... the new man ... right?" The Lieutenant asked.

Myers knew to play it safe until he learned more. "Yes Sir."

"Good!" the Lieutenant smiled. "You learn quickly. Do you want to know why none of these men tried to attack me just now?"

"I don't know Sir."

"Because if any of them even try ... they all will pay for it." the Lieutenant told him. "If anyone attacks me here none of them will eat all day or the next day and the man ... or men that did the attacking will die ..." the Lieutenant stepped closer to Myers. "... will die ... over a few days. They will die slowly and right out there in front of the others. You'll hear their screams all day and night until I finally have them shot."

Myers made a sad face and looked down. The Lieutenant continued saying; "You want to attack me"

"No Sir." Myers quickly answered. His sad look was a fake one trying to appear submissive to the Lieutenant.

Choe turned and left the building with his guards behind him. The men got into a line so Myers did the same. "Now we eat." someone behind Myers said. He looked back but could not tell who said it. When the line started moving Myers moved with it. Before long he found himself outside with the line leading to a table.

On the table were large pots with steam coming from them. The first man in the line picked up a bowl and stuck it out to the man behind the table. A glob of rice was dumped into the man's bowl and he left for some tables that had been set up. When Myers stepped up to get his rice the man behind the table dumped a glob of rice into his bowl.

"So you're the cook." Myers said as he turned to walk away.

"Ha!" the cook said. "I work with what I am given."

Myers did not even look back at the cook as he did not mean to insult him anyway. He knew that the cook was probably not given good food to work with and yet he still gave them nourishment for the day.

"Here!" a man said. "Sit here." It was Rand; the man that held the candle the night before.

Myers sat down and picked up the gummy ball of rice. After letting out a heavy sigh he took a bite. Not even a little bit of salt was used in the rice so the flavor had a great deal to be desired.

"So what happens next?" Myers asked Rand.

"Hurry up and eat." Rand said as he took the last bite of his rice. "We are working to build the warehouses until just before dark."

"Then what?"

"We're taken back to the barracks."

"Do they feed us anymore?" Myers asked as the ball of rice that he was working on was not very much.

"They feed us again around noon and just before going back to the barracks but it is the same old rice." a man across the table said. On Sundays we work all day and are given better rice before going back to the barracks. Sometimes we even get some soup but don't expect any meat to be in it. They boil bones and add some vegetables to it and then call it soup."

"Yeah!" another man said. "It is Choe's way of rewarding us for a week of good work."

"You work all week for that one good meal." Rand added. "Oh and one more thing too ... that Sunday evening you can go back for seconds but that is all."

What makes the rice better on Sundays?" Myers asked.

"They add salt to the rice when they make it." another man said.

"Alright." a North Koran soldier yelled. "Lets go."

The men at the table stood and turned to face the soldier so Myers did the same. Then armed Korean soldiers lead them out to the warehouse construction site where the men knew what they were suppose to be doing.

"You." a North Korean Sergeant yelled. "You're the new one. Come with me."

The Sergeant took Myers to a tool room where he was put with another prisoner to hand out tools to the workers. "You work here." the Sergeant said to Myers locking the door to the tool room behind Myers.

"I'm Larry Sanders." the other man said. "I guess they put you in here to help me lift the heavier tools."

Larry was an older man of about sixty years and was unable to handle the heavier tools like ninety pound jackhammers and so on. He taught Myers the job and how that he had to write each tool down along with the man's name that got it. At the end of the day the list had to be cleared showing that all tools were brought back before any of the men were allowed to eat.

"Why are you in here?" Myers asked Larry.

"The soldiers broke into my home one night and took me away. Probably all of us are from Franklin ... taken from our homes by force for no reason at all." Then he looked at Myers and asked; "What's your story?"

"Me and some ..." He did not know if he could trust Larry so he did not tell the true story. "... some friends were traveling through Texas to Free America when I was captured. The others were killed."

"We have a few men in here that were captured while fighting the Koreans." Larry said as he handed a tool to one of the men outside. "They were given a choice to work here or be executed."

Larry and Myers spent the rest of the day learning things from each other. When the day ended Larry showed Myers how to check the list and make sure that all of the tools were returned. When the door was unlocked Larry handed the list to the North Korean Sergeant and told him that all of the tools had been returned. Then they got in line for the evening meal.

When Larry and Myers went back into the barracks they found out that their bunks were right across from each other.

"When did you come in?" Larry asked Myers.

"Yesterday evening."

"Wow!" Larry said. "We were let off work early because a Korean soldier got hurt but I must have been out of it."

"What are you saying?"

""I must have been sound asleep." Larry replied. "I don't remember seeing you come in."

"It was dark when they brought me in." Myers told Larry. "Rand showed me to this bunk."

"Yeah ... Rand is the barracks leader. He is responsible for everything that happens in the barracks."

Both men fell asleep and Myers finished his first day but around midnight he woke up to a disturbance outside. He started to get up and look out the window but Larry advised him to stay in bed.

"Sometimes they shoot anyone standing at the windows at night." Larry said.

Myers lay back down and as the noise outside vanished he fell asleep again. That night he dreamt of the Ghost Warriors and especially Jenifer. He never told her how he felt about her. Suddenly the lights turned on and the trashcan was thrown down the walkway again. Myers was starting his second day as a prisoner of the North Koreans.

After eating Larry and Myers were taken to the tool room. The door was locked behind them. Myers noticed that the Korean Sergeant always believed what Larry told him about all of the tools being returned. He began to plan an escape.

"You ever thought about escaping?" Myers asked Larry.

"Many times but I'm to old to run anymore."

"I was just wondering ... why you never tried." Myers said. "With all of these tool here you should have no problem." Myers advised.

"Well I'll tell you what." Larry said with a big smile. "If you're planning something and you can handle me being a little slower than you then ... I'm in."

Myers and Larry planned their escape for over a week. The hard part was getting out of the barracks after it was locked up. Larry said that some of the men might even start yelling rather than excepting punishment for anyone escaping. Choe would surely punish all of them if anyone even tried to escape.

One night Myers noticed that the window at the far end of the barracks was left unlocked. A man could open it and slide through to the ground unnoticed. The problem was being quiet enough that the other men did not start yelling out.

That day Myers grabbed a pair of wire cutters and slipped them into his pocket. Larry saw him do it but did not care. He knew that it was just part of the plan to get through the two fences. That evening Larry and Myers walked out of the tool room and Larry handed the list to the Sergeant as if nothing had changed. If Myers got caught with the wire cutters Larry would pretend that he did not know. There was no reason for him to die also.

When Myers got to his bunk he lay down and slipped the wire cutters out of his pocket. As he held the wire cutters between his leg and the wall he looked around. He had already found a slit in the mat he lay on so he slipped the wire cutters into the mat. No one but he and Larry knew that he had the wire cutters.

After everyone was asleep Myers got up and tested his ability to open the window without waking anyone up. As he walked by some of the men he could hear the floorboards creak but the other men were so tired that no one woke up. Finally he was at the window. As he opened the window the man in the top bunk to his right spoke.

"They'll shot anyone looking out of a window at night you know." His voice woke others up.

"You know what Choe will do to us if anyone escapes?" another man asked.

By then almost everyone was awake. "I was just looking outside." Myers pleaded. "I can't sleep."

"Close the window or you'll get us all in trouble." another man said. "You're new here so listen to us and we'll keep you out of trouble."

Myers closed the window and went back to his bunk. He lay there trying to think of another plan but nothing came to him. He finally fell back to sleep just in time for the lights to come on and the usual trash can rolling down the walkway.

Myers and Larry got up and looked at each other. Larry had been awake during the entire time that Myers was up at the window and knew what happened. Neither man said a thing. They would be able to talk after being locked in the tool room.

After eating all of the men were taken to the construction site. Before Larry and Myers were locked in the tool room a Korean soldier grabbed Myers' arm.

"Come with me." the Korean soldier said as he locked Larry in the tool room and lead Myers away.

The Korean soldier held onto Myers' arm until they came to the office building. This building held all of the offices for the Chinese and Korean officers and a couple of sergeants. The soldier lead Myers to an office down the hall and sat him in a chair. In front of Myers was a large desk with a very elegant chair behind it. A few minutes later he heard the door behind him open and then close. He could hear footsteps coming around to his left side. Then someone sat in the chair across the desk from him. It was Captain Choe.

"How are you doing Mister … Myers is it?" Choe asked.

"I guess I'm okay Sir."

"I have a problem Myers." Choe said. "One of the soldiers said that he saw you looking out one of the barracks windows last night."

"Yes Sir." Myers said as he tried to look obedient. "The other men told me what could happen if I was seen looking out of a window at night so I closed the window and went back to bed."

"Then problem solved." the captain said. "But keep in mind that you'll be shot at that window next time."

"I know Sir." Myers said as he looked down.

Captain Choe told the Korean soldier something and then Myers felt a hand tugging at his arm. He stood and the Korean soldier took him back to the tool room. When the door was unlocked he went inside. The door was locked behind him.

"So what happened?" Larry asked.

"One of the guards saw me at the window last night." Myers confessed. "I think we need to change our plans."

Myers and Larry did not say much the rest of the day. Neither could think of another way to escape. By the end of the day both men were totally depressed. It looked like they would both be getting out of that place but now a few of the other prisoners were keeping them from escaping.

After eating that evening Larry and Myers talked as they walked back to the barracks. Larry asked Myers where the wire cutters were in case he had to escape alone. Myers told him that they were hidden in his mat on his bed. The two laughed and continued to walk back to the barracks.

That night Myers worried about Larry's question on where the wire cutters were. Something was not right so when he sat on his bunk he slipped the wire cutters into his pants pocket. With everyone walking around he walked over to

Larry's bunk and sat down. Larry was taking a shower; something they all took turns doing. Myers talked with a couple of the men there who did not notice that he had torn the mat on Larry's bunk. Then he leaned back and slipped the wire cutters inside Larry's mat.

A few minutes later Larry walked up and Myers stood. They talked for a while and Myers went back to his bunk. He still worried about Larry asking that question but now he felt safe. If Larry was planning to turn him in he would not be the one getting in trouble.

It was quiet that night with a few jets flying over every now and then. Once in a while Myers could hear the Korean soldiers outside walking around and talking. Even with these few distractions Myers got plenty of sleep that night.

The next morning Larry and Myers were awaken in the usual manner. As they walked to get their usual bowl of gummy rice a Korean soldier grabbed Larry's arm. Then the soldier escorted him to the office building. The Sergeant locked Myers inside the tool room and walked away. About an hour later the Sergeant opened the door and ordered Myers out. Another one of the workers went inside the tool room and the door was locked.

Myers was lead to the office building and into Captain Choe's office. As he sat down in the chair he heard the door open again. Looking behind him he saw Choe walk in with Larry behind him. Before he knew it he had armed Korean soldiers standing on both sides of him.

"Do you know why you are here Mister Myers?" the Captain asked.

"No Sir ... I don't."

"As we talk your bunk is being searched for some missing wire cutters." Choe said. "You know anything about them?"

"No Sir." Myers said as he looked over at Larry to his left. "What's going on Larry?"

"He ordered me to watch you ... said he would set me free for doing it." Larry told Myers.

"Shut up." Choe ordered Larry. Then he turned his

attention back to Myers. "So you don't know about any missing tools?"

"No Sir ... we hand the list to the Sergeant every evening."

At that time a few Korean soldiers walked in and one of them handed a pair of wire cutters to Choe. They talked with Choe for a while and then stood by the door. Choe sat in his chair and sighed heavily.

"I trusted you and you did this to me." Choe said.

"I did what Sir?" Myers asked.

"Not you." Choe said. Then he looked at Larry and held up the wire cutters. "I was talking to you Larry."

"What's going on here?" Larry asked as the soldiers grabbed his arms.

"These cutters were found in your bunk not his." Choe said angrily. Then he looked at the two soldier holding Larry's arms and said; "Take him out and shoot him."

"You set me up Myers." Larry yelled as he was drug away. "You set me up."

"He probably blamed you on having the wire cutters to throw any attention away from himself." Choe told Myers. "Go back to work." he added and then told another solder to take him back to the tool room.

As Myers was taken back to the tool room a gunshot rang out across the construction site. When the tool room door was opened the man in there was ordered out and Myers took his place. The door being locked behind him secured him inside. Now he had to plan another escape but, for now he had to allow things to cool down.

For the rest of the day and during the evening meal none of the other men would talk to Myers. They blamed him on Larry's death. After going back to the barracks two of the men tried to jump Myers but he was well able to take care of himself.

"Listen you sons of a bunch of whores ..." Myers said as he was very angry. "... he tried to set me up by telling Choe that I had the missing wire cutters but he had them. Soldiers found them in his bunk mat not mine. Larry killed himself."

The men that were close to Myers backed off a little. "We didn't know that." Rand said.

"Maybe before convicting a man here you should ask a few questions." Myers yelled at the others.

Myers went to his bunk and lay down as did most of the others. Although the others believed Myers' story they knew Larry much longer and liked him very much. It was just hard to trust the new guy.

After eating the morning meal Myers started to walk to the tool room but a Korean soldier grabbed him and took him to the back of the construction site. He was put with three others cleaning up a pile of broken concrete and bricks. The other three had shovels but Myers was not given one. He started picking up large chunks of the concrete and throwing them in the back of a truck. Suddenly he was hit in the back by one of the shovels.

Myers fell to the ground and looked up to see that one of the men was about to swing his shovel to hit him again. He raised his foot just in time for the shovel handle to hit the bottom of his foot. The shovel almost vibrated out of the man's hand. Myers looked at the other two men who were just watching the show. Myers kicked the knee of the man holding the shovel and broke it. The man fell to the ground in pain. Myers grabbed the shovel and swung at the man's head killing him instantly.

Myers quickly turned to face the other two men but they only stood there. At that time a Korean soldier opened a gate so he could come in and stop the fighting. The gate was only seven feet away from Myers so he rushed the gate and the soldier coming through. He slammed the gate on the soldier and grabbed his AK-47. A rifle butt against the soldier's face knocked him out. Myers ran for his life and disappeared into the trees on the west side of the construction site.

There were not that many trees in the group of trees where Myers ran and it was completely surrounded by Korean soldiers in seconds. Myers hid in the middle of a pile of old dead trees that had been pushed together by a bulldozer. As he heard the soldiers working their way through the trees he took aim at one of the soldiers. Suddenly there was a gunshot behind him and Myers fell to the ground. A North Korean soldier behind Myers saw him and fired. The bullet passed through the back of Myers' head killing him before he hit the ground.

Chapter 8

Jenifer's Quest

The Ghost Warriors continued to run away from the bridge not knowing that a platoon of North Korean soldiers were fallowing them. Once they came to an old camp they used earlier they stopped. Jenifer set out three guards a few hundred yards behind them to watch for anyone that might be fallowing. Before Jenifer could get back to the camp gunfire started behind her.

Jenifer ordered a few of the Ghost Warriors to check things out. A few minutes later there was more gunfire. Jenifer could tell that there were many of the enemy fallowing them and she was not going to send anyone else out to be killed. Knowing that the others had to have been killed or captured she took the remaining Ghost Warriors farther to the east.

The Ghost Warriors lost five people that evening; Mike and Britney Barns, Lieutenant Bolinski, and Mark and Janet Jackson. The Ghost Warriors were back down to just five members including young Brent.

Brent took Jenifer's decision to leave his parents behind hard. "You did not even know if they were dead or not." Brent yelled at Jenifer.

"Keep your voice down." Jenifer tried to quiet him some but Brent could not care less.

"I'll yell if I want to." he insisted.

Corporal Tads grabbed Brent by the front of his shirt and almost lifted him off of the ground. "You'll shut your fuck'n mouth or I'll hit you so hard you'll have gray hair when you wake up." Then Tads let Brent fall to the ground and walked away.

Jenifer gave Ann a look suggesting that she tried to calm Brent down. Ann walked over to Brent and put her arms around him. Then he broke down crying.

"He just doesn't understand and he is hurting." Tads told Jenifer.

"I know but ... we only have five of us left ... with him." Jenifer held back a tear.

Tads saw that tear anyway and put his arms around her. "It's going to be okay Jenifer." he told her. "Why don't you go off and talk to God again. He does seem to hear you."

Tads started to let Jenifer go but she held tight. "Don't let go." she begged.

"I know how powerful you are when you pray." Tads said as he pointed at a large log not far away. "Why don't we both go over there and pray together."

Jenifer and Tads walked over to the log and sat down together with their backs to everyone else. Tads held her tight as they prayed. Then Tads seemed to takeover the prayer.

"It's me again God. Jenifer really needs your help. We just lost half of our group and everyone seems to be falling apart. Give us strength Lord. Please give all of us the strength that we need to do what we must do. But most of all help Jenifer here. She is our leader and she needs your guidance. Amen."

Tads and Jenifer continued to sit there on that long for a while holding each other. At one point they looked at each other and then kissed. It was a gentle and tender touch of the lips; quiet but very meaningful. From that point on they held each other closer.

"I'm scared Tads." Jenifer said.

"Why?"

"Every time I start to like someone they get killed or captured."

"Well ... I believe that God has work for me to do so ... I don't think I'll die yet." he told her.

The two kissed again and then stood and went back to the others. Jenifer sat on another log beside her sister.

"Did I see some lip action back there?" Ann asked her

sister. "You can get diseases that way you know."

"And just what disease is that?" Jenifer asked.

Ann leaned over to Jenifer and whispered in her ear; "You can get … a man."

"You idiot." Jenifer said as she pushed her sister not knowing that everyone was listening. "I thought you were serious."

Everyone started laughing shocking and embarrassing Jenifer. She stood and walked away. As she stepped out into the darkness the others stopped laughing. When Tads was able to stop smiling he also stood and fallowed Jenifer into the darkness of the night.

Tads found Jenifer with one of the people she sent out to watch for any troops that might be fallowing their tracks. With the river still being flooded there was no way to keep from making tracks in the mud.

"I'm sure that someone could be and … probably is fallowing us." Jenifer told Tads as he walked up to her.

"I'm sure that more North Korean soldiers came to help the others and were probably fallowing our tracks in the mud until it got dark." Tads told Jenifer. "We really should keep moving in the night."

"There's no moon for light to walk by." Jenifer reminded Tads.

"We still need to get out of here even if we have to feel our way."

Jenifer was thinking and knew that Tads was right. She told Leo who was watching their back to fallow them back to the camp. Once there she ordered everyone to get ready to move out. When all of the Ghost Warriors were ready Jenifer lead them farther east.

By time the Ghost Warriors reached their favorite hiding spot just southeast of Marquez they were all tired. Jenifer decided to allow everyone to rest for a few days. She and Tads talked for a while trying to think of what they could do.

"What can we do now with only five of us … one of which is a boy?" Jenifer asked Tads.

"Brent is eighteen years old ... a man by any standards."

"Yeah I know." Jenifer said. "It's just that he looks so much younger."

"Maybe someday we can use that."

"I still don't know what to do." Jenifer put her face in her hands. "I'm not my father."

"Maybe you should stop trying to do things the way the Mountain Ghost would do them ... and start doing things the way the Mountain Ghost's daughter would do them."

Jenifer looked up at Tads. He was right but how would she do things? As she wonder she asked Tads.

"I don't know Jenifer." Tads told her. "Pray about it and ask God to show you ... your way."

With that Tads stood and walked away. Jenifer thought for a moment and then stood. After looking around at the others she left camp for a little privacy. After finding a large log she sat down and thought about how she should do things. How can she be like her father without doing things like her father would?

"Father ... Tads was right. I do need to start doing things my way. Every time I try doing things the way my father might do it I fail. Please Lord ... show me ... my way to do things. Show me what you want me to do."

For a long time Jenifer sat on that log. It began to rain again but she did not move. When she noticed that the wind shifter out of the northwest she knew that a cold front was on its way so she got up and went back to camp. By time she go to the camp everyone already had their rain gear on or was putting it on. She wasted no time getting hers on as well.

It got bitterly cold that night. The rain turned into a freezing rain and by morning everything was covered in ice. Snow started to fall and continued throughout the day. Knowing that everyone was very cold Jenifer told Brent to start a campfire. The Korean soldier did not usually checkout campfires but the black drones did. However; they had not seen any black drones for about two weeks.

Twice during the day chunks of snow fell through the trees and put out the campfire. To reduce the chances of being caught Jenifer had everyone keep the fire low. It did not take much falling snow to put the campfire out. Restarting the fire was not easy. Fresh and dry kindling had to be found to start the fire again. Then dry wood had to be found and the group of trees that they hid in was not all that big. Jenifer did not want anyone moving around during the day.

All through the day Jenifer continued to ask God to help her but she got no answers as to what she should do. Then finally she got an idea but was not sure she liked it. Her father and his friend Wu did many things just by themselves. She remembered her father telling her and Ann about all they did. The Mountain Ghost and a friend named Wu did almost everything as ghost snipers as they picked off enemy soldiers. Maybe that was what she had to do.

A few minutes later Jenifer stood before the other four Ghost Warriors. She looked them over and then called their attention. When they had all put aside what they were doing and were listening to her she spoke to them.

"I have prayed and decided that I will go alone to a place that has not yet been decided. Ann will be in charge and I want her to take you all back to the burned home of a man that was a friend of our father. It was the home of Tom and a place where God delivered our father out of the hands of the enemy. Wait for me there."

When Jenifer finished the others jumped up and tried to get her to change her mind but she stood fast on her decision. Jenifer walked over and got all of her gear, dawned her backpack and put her rain poncho over it. Then she grabbed her 270 rifle and looked at everyone again. After giving everyone a hug Jenifer left the camp.

The sun was just coming up. As Jenifer walked off she had no idea where she was going or what she was going to do. She gave a quick prayer asking God to lead her. Then she got an idea. She would head back to the anti-aircraft guns just west of

Marquez and act as a sniper. She would terrorize the North Koreans by killing one at a time; maybe one that day and another that night. She would wear the white paste and tear her cloths so she would look like something that crawled out of a grave. It had been a long time since the Mountain Ghost or the ghost of anything terrorized the enemy. She was going to start it again.

It took two days for Jenifer to work her way around Marquez and to the fuel depot two miles west of the town. By this time she was on the east side of Highway 79 and in a thin line of trees south of the depot. Late in the evening she took aim at a North Korean soldier in one of the guard towers and fired. With the silencer that she had on her rifle the shot was not heard. With it getting dark she took aim at the guard in another guard tower and fired again. This soldier fell out of the tower and other soldiers then knew that someone was shooting at them.

Jenifer took advantage of the confusion and darkening skies and slipped out of the area. She worked her way to a large group of trees farther south of the depot to rest. She would not make another hit until later the next day.

Jenifer rested that night in the group of trees but, it was cold. At least the snow and freezing rain had stopped. Later that night as she shivered in the cold she was awaken to the sound of a black drone flying overhead. It was a good thing that she had not built a fire to stay warm.

Jenifer slowly grabbed her rifle and got ready to fire if she had to but, staying quiet and hidden was more important. She saw her job for the time being as a ghost that popped up every now and then and shot a Korean soldier. The black drone flew on by and continued on its way not even knowing that she was there. She thought to herself; *Thank God they don't have infer red on them.* The larger drone did have infer red cameras on them but they only flew at night.

Jenifer could not sleep the rest of the night. She had never been alone before and she was scared. She was not scared of making any mistakes but of just being alone. If anything happened to her no one would know. No one would know where to find her body so they could not bury her. Her body would be torn apart by wild animals and her bones scattered through the woods and nearby fields. Then again; she was a Christian and her soul would be in Heaven so why should she care what happened to her body?

"Help me Father. Please go with me and lead me. Please give me the strength I need to do this."

Jenifer took a deep breath and let it out in a heavy sigh. Then she noticed that her fears were gone. She felt so confident in herself and she knew that she was going to be successful at what she had set out to do. *Thank you Father;* she thought to herself.

As the light of the next day began to show Jenifer the area around her she noticed a North Korean patrol walking towards her. Had the black drone seen her and she did not know it? Were the soldiers coming to get her? She got as low as she could and got ready for a fight. With her having a bolt action rifle she knew it would not be much of a fight but she had no choice.

The Korean patrol walked right up to the trees only fifteen feet from Jenifer. Then they turned and walked towards the east without even looking into the trees where Jenifer was. She was well hidden and they would have never seen her until they probably stepped on her but that did not make her feel any better. The patrol walking away and that made her feel much better though.

Because of the fear that she had felt only seconds earlier Jenifer lay back down on her back. As she looked through the trees above her she saw a falling star. She thanked God for showing her the star and took it as a message to get out of there. Something told her to leave the area.

Jenifer got up and started moving deeper into the trees. She crossed a small unused road and into the trees farther to the southeast. She lay down and waited until it was daylight again so she could see around.

Jenifer started using the white paste to look like a ghost but she had to leave the area as quickly after firing her rifle as she could. She was to close to her targets. She would have to start picking targets farther away so that she could stand and allow the enemy to see her as a ghost. Then she could leave the area.

When it was daylight enough to see around her Jenifer walked around the trees that she was in and saw a short distance away a larger group of trees. Traveling there during the daylight would be risky but she had to do it. Moving to the most southern end of the trees where she was gave her a clear shot to the other trees. Within an hour she had made it to the other group of trees and was looking for a good place to fire from.

This group of trees was shaped much like a diamond. At the northern point two smaller lines of trees branched off towards the northwest and the northeast. This gave her two firing positions to fire from and both were at least three hundred yards away from the depot fence.

The northeastern fork of trees also gave her a thin tree line to the east where she could cross Highway 7 and move to a larger group of trees to the north of the depot. However; this group of trees would put her to close to the depot. They were right on the highway and across the highway from the depot itself. If she fired from these trees she would have to do it from the eastern end of the tree line.

Jenifer chose the western fork to fire from late that evening. She slowly moved through the trees so she would not be seen. Then she set up to fire at the southwestern guard tower. After applying the white paste to any exposed skin she pulled her knife and cut her clothing a little more. Rubbing in a little of the mud help to complete the look of a dead person.

Jenifer had to choose a time when the sun was up enough for the soldiers to see a ghost but low enough to give her quick coming darkness so she could run and hide. When the time was right she lay down in the prone position and put the butt of her rifle against her right shoulder. After sliding her left fist under the rifle butt she looked through the scope.

The Korean soldier in the southwestern tower was just standing there giving her a perfect, non-moving target. She flipped the safety off and continued to aim. Then she took a deep breath and let it out. As soon as she pulled the trigger the soldier fell to the floor of the tower. She took aim at the soldier in the southeastern tower and fired. He also fell but the Koreans at the depot still did not know that anything was wrong.

The silencer on Jenifer's 270 rifle was doing a great job but she needed the Koreans at the depot to know that their men were being killed so she aimed at a soldier standing by the barracks. This time when she fired and the soldier fell she knew that she got their attention.

As whistles blew and Korean soldiers ran Jenifer stood in plane sight. She held her rifle at chest level and yelled as loud as she could. Her blood curdling cry stopped almost all movement in the depot compound. As the Korean soldiers looked at the ghost she gave another blood curdling yell and then slowly lowered herself to the ground. Once on the ground she crawled away as quickly as she could.

Jenifer made her way back to the larger group of trees to the south and then she went farther into the trees to hide. Then she fallowed these trees to the west and waited. She was far enough away that she felt safe and decided to rest until it got dark.

When it was dark enough to move Jenifer crossed Highway 7 and into the large group of trees. This group of trees was northwest of the depot and came to a point that pointed to the southeast; right at the depot. She would use this point of the trees for her next attack.

That night Jenifer rested. It was cold but she could build no fire to help keep her warm. As the temperature dropped and the misty rain turned to snow she slid over to a tall cedar tree and pulled some dead limbs together to form a small lean-to. Then she cut a few of the green limbs and piled them against the walls of the lean-to. It did not keep her any warmer but it kept the snow off of her.

When Jenifer woke up she noticed that the sun was already turning the eastern sky a baby blue color. The ground was covered with snow and she knew that moving around would leave tracks but, she had to do something. Moving quickly but watching out for anyone walking around she finally made it to where she would fire from. After setting up just back a little in the trees she put on her white paste.

The morning sun was just over Jenifer's right shoulder so she would have to make sure that they saw her. She took aim at the guard in the western tower and pulled the trigger. Again no one heard the shot thanks to the silencer on her rifle. She took aim at the guard in the northwestern tower and fired. Like the first one he also fell to the floor of the tower.

The two guard towers at the gate were a farther shot but she figured that she could make the shot. She took aim at the guard in the northern tower and fired. The bullet ricocheted off of the post beside the guard's face. He ducked and yelled. Then an alarm went off and all of the Korean soldiers in the depot compound started running around. But with her having the silencer on her rifle they still did not know where the shot came from. As the guard in the northern tower showed his head she took aim again. This time when she pulled the trigger the Korean soldier fell.

By this time the sun's rays were shining through the trees so she stood and held her rifle above her head. Then she gave that blood curdling scream that sent chills all over the soldiers in the compound. AK-47s starting firing at her but they were not even coming close. She just slowly backed up into the darkness of the trees and vanished. Wasting no time she quickly headed to the most northern part of the group of trees and rested.

Jenifer knew that the Koreans would be sending out patrols covering large areas around the depot so she decided to get out of the area. She fallowed the trees until she found a thin line of trees heading to the northwest. Then she fallowed them into a very large group of trees and took them as far as she could to the north. When the darkness of the night came she stopped and rested for the night.

Jenifer woke up a few hours before daylight and with a full moon she headed towards the east. She wanted to get back to the others. By time the sky started showing some color she realized that she was close to the town of Marquez. She turned north until she found some more tree cover and crossed Highway 79.

As Jenifer crossed Highway 79 about three miles north of Marquez a motor patrol spotted her and quickly went to where she crossed. As the Korean soldiers pilled out of the truck backup was called for. Within thirty minutes three more trucks loaded with Korean soldiers arrived. Jenifer had no idea that she had been seen and that two companies of well armed North Korean soldiers were behind her.

Suddenly Jenifer heard a gunshot behind her. She looked back and saw that the woods were full of little brown uniforms. She began to run. With it now being daylight there would be no hiding in the darkness. Then she came to a deep gully. It was not very wide so she tried to jump to the other side. As she jumped sharp pain in her right leg caused her to land at the bottom of the gully. That was when she saw that she had been shot in the right leg just above the knee.

Jenifer could hear the Korean soldiers yelling and, as they got closer she knew she had to do something quick. She started running the best that she could towards the north. This would take her farther away from the others but most of the Korean soldiers seemed to be to the south. As she ran up the gully the sounds of the Korean soldiers seemed to disappear.

Jenifer finally came to a washout that came into the gully. She took it out of the gully and headed back to the east. By time it started to get dark she was very tired and the bullet would in her leg was still bleeding. She tore a strip from her shirt and wrapped it around the wound to stop the bleeding. Then she set against a tree to allow the wound to clot. She knew that if she continued to walk she would bleed to death.

Jenifer slept all night not waking up one time. When she did wake up the sun was already up. At first she could not move but as she worked on it she limbered up some. It took a while but she was finally able to walk but, very slowly. She picked up an old oak tree limb and used it as a cane. It helped a great deal.

It was a slow go but by noon Jenifer came to a spot that she recognized. She was not far from the others but she was very tired and sat down to rest. Her leg was bleeding again so she tore another strip from her shirt and replaced the old bandage on her leg. Not realizing just how weak she was she fell asleep.

Jenifer woke up just after midnight. With a clear sky and full moon she was able wake up enough to travel. Her leg hurt and was still stiff after not moving for a while but she stood and tried. The more she moved the easier it got. Before long she was walking; slow but still walking.

When Jenifer got to the meeting place where the others were suppose to be she found no one there. *Where could they have gone?* she thought to herself. *Where are they?*

Chapter 9

The Search

Jenifer looked around the meeting area for any hints as to where everyone went. There was no sign of a fight or struggle of any kind so, they had to have left on their own. Or could they have been chased away by someone? Had Korean soldiers come through and found them? Had they maybe been captured? There were so many questions and no answers. The main question was, what should she do now?

"I'm in a fix again Father. I don't know what to do. Were the others captured or just chased out of here? Did they get tired of waiting on me and left for someplace else? I don't even know which direction they went. Help me Lord. Please help me."

Jenifer sat on a log and looked around. If God was going to show her something then she would have to stop and look for it. Then she noticed a trail leading out of the camp. It was one that had been used many times by them and animals but this time it looked more wore down. She got up and walked over to the trail. Sure enough there were fresh boot prints in the mud. The others had headed to the east, towards Centerville and it had not been long.

The mud on the trail had dried a little to a thin crust but in the boot prints the mud was still wet. That meant that the others must have left the camp just a few hours before she got there. Jenifer checked her leg and had to replace the wrap over her wound. Her shirt was getting smaller by the day. Then she got her gear and took the trail towards Centerville.

The farther Jenifer walked the more she found that proved that the others went that way as well. She only hoped that the others were not wanting to actually go into Centerville. As she walked farther she started hearing the sound of vehicles on the move. Taking her time to get closer she found that somehow she had turned to the south and was standing close to Highway 7. It was still daylight so she did not want to get so close that she would be seen.

Just before the sun went down Jenifer crept out on the side of the highway. She looked to the north and saw nothing so she looked to the south. On the next hill were what looked like a company of North Korean soldiers setting up camp. Two tanks were also there on the southern side of the highway. It was getting to dark to take any shots so she went back into the woods and sat down beside a large oak tree. She was almost excited and could not fall asleep so she went back to the edge of the trees beside the highway.

Jenifer lay there under a few cedar branches she cut and pulled over herself. As she watched the figures walking around the three campfires that they had she wondered what they could be doing. Were they still looking for her? They would not have captured the others and then stopped so close to Centerville. Then not meaning to do so she fell asleep.

Jenifer woke up when two North Korean soldiers walked by her on the highway and stopped just feet in front of her. She could not move or she would be seen. The moon was not full but the moonlight left her in the shadows of an overhanging tree. *God help me* she thought to herself.

One of the Korean soldiers walked over to Jenifer and stood over her not knowing that she was even there. Then he unzipped his pants and did something that Jenifer knew would be coming. A few seconds later the soldiers continued their rounds never knowing that they were so cloze to her. When they were far enough away Jenifer crawled back into the trees and stood. With the smell of urine all over her she suddenly did not want to find the others anytime soon.

Jenifer thanked God when she heard thunder off to the southeast. That usually meant rain was coming and she needed a shower bad. When she got back to the spot where she had been earlier she sat down against the oak tree. She checked her leg and fell asleep again.

A sudden flash of lightening and loud thunder woke Jenifer up. As the rain started to fall she stood allowing the fresh water to clean her. Knowing that she was alone she stripped her clothes off and hung them on branches to allow the rain to clean them as well. As she stood there in the rain she held her rifle ready for anyone to walk up.

The rain came down hard for many hours but stopped just as quickly as it started. The clouds cleared out and the morning sun brightened the area. Jenifer got dressed, put on her white paste, and walked out to the highway and looked both directions. The company of Korean soldiers were still about half a mile to the east. She lay down and extended the bipod on her rifle.

A soldier was standing on top of one of the tanks making himself a perfect target. Jenifer took aim and fired. A split second later the soldier fell to the ground. Suddenly there was so much action in the Korean camp that Jenifer could not keep up with them. When she noticed another soldier on the top of the same tank she took aim again and fired. *Another Korean bites the dust.* She thought to herself.

The Koreans still had no idea where the shots were coming from but with them encamped on the western side of a hill the shots could not have been coming from the east. An officer stood and ordered soldiers to run down the highway to the west. Jenifer took aim at the officer and fired. He fell dead. Then she stood and gave her soon to be famous blood curdling scream. As the soldiers stopped and fired she knew that she was out of range of their AK-47s and gave another scream. Then she slowly vanished into the trees.

Once Jenifer was in the trees she picked up her pace. She knew that the Korean soldiers would be on her soon. Suddenly there was an explosion in front of her. The tanks were firing wildly into the woods hoping to hit the ghost. She turned and headed off to the northwest hopefully to get out of the rang of the tank fire. As she ran the explosions continued to drop around her. Finally the tanks stopped firing. *The Korean soldiers must be in the woods now.*

With her leg bleeding again and hurting bad Jenifer slowed her pace to a quick walk. After about half a mile she stopped to rest. Knowing that if she sat down her leg might stiffen again she rested on her feet taking a few steps every now and then. When she was rested enough she continued walking faster to the north.

After slowly making her way another half mile Jenifer collapsed. She could run no more. Laying there in the mud she asked God for help.

"Father ... Father ... Why have you brought me here? Why have you left me so weak that I can't move? Please help me Father."

At that moment Jenifer passed out from blood loss and exhaustion. Later she woke up enough to feel someone moving her but she could not open her eyes. She passed out again.

Before Jenifer and Ann even came down to central Texas Lieutenant Colonel Haung had stopped all walking on the highways between towns except for those traveling to and from the Weekend Trade Day in Centerville. Although he continued to allow this he mainly did it so that he and his soldiers could keep an eye out for anyone that was wanted. He also changed the weekend from every weekend to the first and third weekend of every month. This lessened the amount of traveling by the American civilians. Because of this most of the civilians that wanted to do any traveling stayed to the woods and not the roads.

The next time Jenifer woke up she found herself in someone's bed. As she tried to move she gasped at the sudden pain in her leg. She slowly moved the sheet and blanket to look at her leg. It took almost all of her energy just to do that. It looked like the bullet had been removed and the wound was sown up with three stitches.

Mustering up enough energy to call someone she barely asked; "Is anyone there?"

"Just a moment." a woman's voice called back to her.

A few seconds later an old woman walked into the bedroom wiping her hands on a rag. "So you're awake."

"Yes Ma'am." Jenifer was barely able to say.

"You lost a lot of blood but my husband fixed you up." the old woman said. "You just lay there and I'll bring you some soup. You need to build your strength back up."

When the old woman came back with the soup her husband was with her. As the woman fed Jenifer her husband had a few questions.

"Who are you young lady?" he asked.

"My name is Jenifer."

The man shook his head up and down and then told her; "My name is Benny and my wife is Loretta." he told Jenifer.

Benny and Loretta were Mexican Americans that had been in the country legally since before the invasion. "I found you while I was out checking my traps. I brought you here and removed that bullet in your leg. However; you're gon'a be here a while. You lost a lot of blood and you need to build your strength before you leave."

"My rifle." Jenifer was almost passing out again.

"I hid it and your gear in case another Korean patrol comes by." Benny said. "I ... we know who you are."

"... turn me in?" Jenifer tried to ask.

"If we were going to turn you in we would have already done it." Loretta said.

Benny held up the jar of white paste and asked; "Judging by this I would say that you're one of the Ghost Twins ... aren't you?"

"Yes ... I am."

"Well you don't worry about a thing." Loretta said. "We'll take care of you."

As soon as Jenifer finished her bowl of soup she laid back and fell asleep again. It took almost a full week before she had the strength to get out of the bed. Loretta helped her get to the dinner table and around the home for other reasons but she was determined to do things on her own. After two weeks she was moving around the home on her own but she was still weak.

"I need to be moving out soon." Jenifer told Benny and Loretta. "I need to find my sister and the others.

Jenifer had already told Benny and Loretta about the Ghost Warriors and how she just missed them. Finding them now would not be easy but, she had to try. Just as she started to go get her rifle and gear the front door to the home opened and in stepped a Korean Sergeant and a few of his soldiers.

"Howdy Sergeant." Benny said as he turned to face him.

"Mister ... Hawkins." the Sergeant said as he walked past him. Then he looked at Jenifer and asked; "Who is this?"

"She's a friend." Benny quickly answered.

The Sergeant looked Jenifer over closely. "What is your name?"

"Molly ... Sir." she answered quickly. "My name is Molly."

The Sergeant looked her over a few more seconds and then turned his attention back to Benny. "We are looking for a few ... ghosts that have been killing our soldiers."

"I've read in the paper about them but haven't seen any ghosts." Benny said.

The Sergeant looked around saying nothing else. Then he walked outside and the door shut behind the last soldier.

Benny looked at Jenifer and said; "That's the way he does it. He's never here long."

"I think I'll wait a while ... until dark before I leave." Jenifer said. "They should be long gone by then."

Jenifer, Benny and Loretta played Uno at the dinner table as they waited for darkness to come. By time it was dark enough for Jenifer to leave she had realized that she was absolutely terrible at playing Uno. As she stood to get her rifle and gear she made a comment about never playing cards again.

Jenifer slung her backpack on and fastened the two straps. Then she picked up her rifle and walked to the door. Both Benny and Loretta gave her a hug and then she was off. In seconds she had disappeared into the darkness.

There was no moon that night so making her way through the woods was almost impossible. As it started to sprinkle she realized that the moon could have been out but the cloud cover was blocking it. It sprinkled all night until the temperature dropped below freezing. Then the rain turned to sleet and then snow. By time daylight came she was tired and sat beside a tree to rest.

Off in the distance to the east Jenifer could hear explosions. She figured that the American jets were attacking Centerville again. The gentle rumbling from the bombs put her to sleep. She must have been more tired than she thought. By time she woke up the sun was already up.

As the rumbling continued Jenifer started walking towards the sound. By that evening she had made it to the western side of Interstate 45. Laying close to the edge of the trees she covered herself with cedar branches that she cut earlier. As the night went on she fell asleep and woke up a few times. Each time she woke up she looked across the interstate at the action going on. Finally she realized that American soldiers were fighting Korean soldiers on the ground. The explosions were not bombs dropped by American jets but grenades going off.

By time the sun started coming up she was able to aim and shoot a few Korean soldiers. She continued to fire until she only had five rounds left. Not wanting to use the last five rounds that she had she backed up and disappeared into the woods. As she left the area thirteen Korean soldiers lay dead in the western outskirts of Centerville thanks to a 270 rifle with a silencer.

The only ammunition that Jenifer knew of was what was buried in the red barn just southwest of Mexia. There should be three ammo boxes there. She and her sister had buried the ammo cans when they first came to the area and took only what they could carry. She would need to go get all of the 270 ammunition and bring it back to that area. Then she could rebury two of the ammo cans so that she could get to them as she needed them.

Jenifer set out for the red barn. It would be a long travel to the northwest but she could do it. As she walked she would have to avoid any contact with any of the enemy.

While Jenifer traveled to the barn she came upon a home where a North Korean patrol was harassing the home owner. She could only watch as the Korean soldiers beat and kicked the old man and woman. She wanted nothing more than to kill every Korean soldier there but, with only five rounds she knew that she would not survive. She turned her head but could still hear the screams of pain echoing through the trees.

Finally the screaming stopped. Jenifer looked up to see the Korean patrol leaving. On the ground were the old man and woman. As soon as the patrol was out of sight she stood and walked to the old man and woman. They were both dead.

Jenifer found a shovel and buried the two. After digging the grave she lay them side by side and then filled in the grave. Then she went in to the home to take what she could use. To her surprise she saw a box of ammunition sitting on the fireplace mantle. As she looked at the box her eyes got big. The box was that of 270 ammunition but, when she opened the box she found only five rounds in it. She had hoped for a full box but at least she had five more rounds than she had before.

With ten rounds of 270 ammunition Jenifer left the home and continued on her way to the northwest. She saw no more Koreans and reached the barn four days later. For a while she stood in the trees watching the barn to make sure that she was alone. After about thirty minutes she felt safe to go into the barn.

Jenifer opened the barn door and quickly stepped inside closing the door behind her. She stood in the darkness watching to see if there was any movement. After a few minutes she walked over to the left corner. The ammo cans should be about a foot under the ground if no one else had found them.

Before digging Jenifer sat on the ground watching and listening. This barn was to good a shelter for no one to be there. After almost an hour she went ahead and started digging but still kept an eye out for any movement. Finally she got to the first ammo box and pulled it up. When she opened it she saw that the 308 ammunition had been removed. Then she opened the other two ammo cans and found that the 308 ammunition was gone from them as well. That meant that Ann had already been there and got only the ammunition for her M-14 rifle.

Jenifer put all of the 270 ammunition in her back pack and reburied the ammo cans. If Ann came back she wanted to make sure that her sister knew that she had been there and not someone else. Anyone else would take the empty ammo cans. With enough ammunition to start a small war she covered herself with some of the hay laying around and waited to fall asleep.

As Jenifer lay there she wondered if she should go ahead and head back north to Free America. She was only about one hundred fifty miles away anyway. But with her sister still missing she couldn't do that. At least she knew that Ann and probably the others had been there but, when?

Jenifer knew that she had fallowed the others to Centerville and then left there and went straight to the red barn. If the others had gone into Centerville then how could they have made it to the red barn before her? How could they have been there and left before she even got there? The only answer was that she was not fallowing the others to Centerville. She fallowed someone else to Centerville while her sister and the others went to the red barn. Then the big question came to her. Which direction did they go after leaving the barn?

Jenifer woke up later to a rooster crowing. Daylight would be coming soon so she got up and got ready to leave. Then she heard voices coming from the other end of the barn.

"Be quiet. They'll hear you."

Jenifer stood and yelled; "Come out. I have no desire to harm you."

"I'm coming out." a man yelled. "Don't shoot."

"I'm not gon'a shoot but come out unarmed." Jenifer

warned the man.

As the man walked close enough for Jenifer to see him she saw a young man with his hands up. "Stop right there." She calmly said. "What are you doing here?"

"My family and I were burned out of our home last week by a Korean patrol." the man advised. "We have been trying to get to Free America and just spent the night in here. We'll leave … if you let us."

Jenifer lowered her rifle. "Like I said … I'm not going to hurt any of you. I only hurt Chinese and Koreans and … a communist sympathizer every now and then."

The man laughed at Jenifer's remark. She stepped closer and shook the man's hand and then advised him on how to get to Free America. "When you get back tell everyone that you met one of the daughters of the Mountain Ghost."

The man's eyes got big. "You're one of he Ghost Twins."

"Yeah … I guess so." Jenifer said with a smile. She always thought that the name Ghost Twins was a funny name. "I'm Jenifer Blake. I'm looking for my sister and a few others with her."

"Is her name Ann?" the man asked.

"Yeah … why?"

They left out of here two evenings ago."

"Which way did the go?" an excited Jenifer asked.

"They headed south but your sister said that they were going to the Marquez area." the man said. "She said something about a North Korean ammo depot."

"It's to well protected." Jenifer replied. "I need to catch them before they get there."

Jenifer shook the man's hand again and left without saying another word. She knew right where to go but she had to catch up with the others before they tried attacking the ammo depot. Then she remembered that it was not an ammo depot but a fuel depot. Did her sister lie to the man on purpose or was there an ammo depot that she did not know about?

Jenifer walked all night but the fuel depot was still a good three or four days away. By morning she was tired and sat under a large cedar tree to rest. As she sat there she heard the Korean language being spoken. She looked through the branches of the cedar tree and saw one North Korean Sergeant giving orders to others dressed in black. Then an interpreter spoke in English. She counted ten dressed in black. *These have to be the New Communist League.* She thought to herself. Jenifer realized that she had walked right upon an enemy camp.

The new communist League were Americans traitors that chose to help the Chinese and North Koreans. They carried AK-47 rifles and did what ever their North Korean superior ordered them to do. This included murdering innocent American citizens. Jenifer wanted so much to kill her a few of these American Communist but that would have to wait until another time. She was out gunned and to close to try it at that time.

"I can't wait to see one of those Blake sisters in my sights." one of the Communist League members said.

Jenifer could see that he was decorated more than the officers and, although an American he was probably an officer.

"Shoot me will you ..." Jenifer whispered to herself. "I'll be seeing you in my sights later ... you liberal communist son of a whore."

For almost three hours she did not move and finally the communist group left. She still waited another fifteen minutes before coming out from under the cedar tree. She wanted to hurry and find her sister but the New Communist League went the same direction that she had to go. Not wanting to run into them again she turned to the west and went a few miles before turning back to the south.

Because of Jenifer's detour it took her four more days to reach the northern side of Marquez. With the darkness of the night coming quickly she headed west to the fuel depot. When it got to dark to see where she was going she stopped and waited until daylight. Incoming clouds blocked any moonlight that might help her to see around her. Later that night it began to rain again.

The rain got harder through the morning. By time Jenifer had reached the eastern anti-aircraft guns a full fledged storm had hit. Although it was not freezing it was still very cold. She had put on her rain gear when the rain started but with how hard it was coming down she wondered if the poncho was enough.

Across the field where Jenifer was at was an old shed. She headed to it hoping for a little shelter. When she got to the shed she realized that the shed would give her just that; a little shelter. The roof had caved in due to years of neglect but she went to the corner and sat down. Most of the roof above that corner was still up but the rain still found its way in. She pulled an old heavy tarp over herself. It kept her dry but she would not be able to watch for anyone.

Jenifer was very tired and fell asleep but woke up later to voices. At least the English language was being used but, could it be some of the Communist League? She slowly raised the tarp and looked out. Then she heard a voice that she thought that she knew. After uncovering her rifle and getting ready for a fight she took a chance.

"Tads?" she said. The voices stopped. "Tads. Is that you?"

"Jenifer?" Tads said as he walked over to her.

By chance Jenifer finally found the others. Tads and Jenifer gave each other a big hug that seemed to last for ever. Then Ann pushed her way between them and gave her sister a hug. The Ghost Warriors were back together.

Chapter 10

Ghost Warrior

Leo, Tads, and Brent got some loose boards and propped them up against the wall and then wrapped the tarp over it. This gave everyone a dry area in which to wait out the storm. Brent was becoming quite the warrior and took the first watch. He stood by the door where the roof was still keeping that area dry.

Jenifer was so tired that she fell asleep again and slept all night. By time she woke up it was daylight but still raining hard. She crawled out from under the tarp and stood. With her rifle in hand she walked over to her sister who was standing watch at that time.

"I hear that you were planning to hit the fuel depot." Jenifer said.

"Nope!" Ann replied. "We were going to hit an underground ammunition depot."

"I don't know about any ammo depot." Jenifer said.

"We heard about it a few days ago but haven't seen it yet." Ann advised. 'It's under ground you know." she added as a joke.

"Where is it?" Jenifer asked.

"It is suppose to be just past the fuel depot ... actually beside it." Ann told her sister.

Jenifer and Ann decided to leave the shed and head north after the rain stopped. Unfortunately; the rain did not stop for two more days. By the next day it had rained so much that a small stream started flowing into the shed. Brent went out into the rain with a broken shovel and dug a small ditch to turn the water before it came inside the shed.

By that evening no one had eaten for three days and when Tads saw a rabbit he threw a board and killed it. They could not build a fire and ate the rabbit raw. At least they had something to eat.

The next day the rain was still coming down in bucket loads. Finally that evening the rain slowed to a heavy sprinkle. By the next morning the rain was over and the sun was coming up. Before the sun got up the Ghost Warriors were out of the shed and heading north. After a few miles they turned west for a few more miles and then turned south.

The Ghost Warriors did not know that they were so close to the northern anti-aircraft guns until two machineguns opened up on them. Instantly Tads was hit in the head. He was dead before he hit the ground. Then Leo and Brent were hit. The massive amount of blood showed Jenifer that they were also dead.

"Ann ... run." Jenifer yelled but she was to late. Ann was hit three times in the back. She also lay in a large pool of blood. Jenifer turned and ran with all she had. After about half a miles she collapsed and cried.

All because she was not paying attention everyone was dead including her sister. Now she was alone.

"Father ... why did you allow this to happen? Now what am I suppose to do? Everyone is dead. Ann is dead."

For a while Jenifer just lay there and cry. She loved her twin sister. Now she had to leave her and the others where they fell. She could not bury them; could not bury her sister. Then her sadness turned to anger.

"Father ... please help me to make my enemies pay for this. I know that you said that vengeance was yours but ... please help me like you helped my dad and his father. Help me to be the next Mountain Ghost. Please help me to become the greatest Ghost there ever was. Help me to be the ... Ghost Warrior."

By time Jenifer stopped praying and crying she lay down under a cedar tree and fell asleep. The ground was wet and cold but she did not seem to notice. Whether it was anger or sadness over loosing her sister it did not matter. From that moment on Jenifer would never be the same. She was going to be fearless; merciless to the enemy. She was going to become a nightmare for all Chinese and North Koreans. She was now a vicious savage. She was the new Mountain Ghost; The Ghost Warrior.

Jenifer woke up the next morning with full intentions on going back to the northern anti-aircraft guns. Before even leaving the safety of the cedar tree she covered all exposed skin with the white paste. Then she checked her rifle. It only held five rounds but it was fully loaded. With the safety on the rifle set to "S" she started walking towards the northern guns.

Before Jenifer could see a thing she heard Koreans talking and laughing. She clicked the safety off and continued walking slowly taking one step at a time. Then she got on the muddy ground and crawled until she could see the Koreans at the guns. When she got close enough to see all of the soldiers at the guns she slowly piled grass in front of her. With her rifle poking out of the grass she took aim at one soldier and fired. The silencer only let her know that a shot was fired.

The soldier fell to the ground. *Four left.* She thought to herself. The other four looked around as one got on a radio and called for help. A second later another Korean fell dead. Then another and then another. The Korean soldier with the radio stood alone looking around. Jenifer noticed that he was not holding his rifle so she stood and screamed her famous blood curdling cry. Full of fear when he saw Jenifer the Korean soldier passed out and fell to the ground. With two trucks full of more soldiers Jenifer backed into the darkness of the trees and vanished.

Jenifer allowed the last Korean soldier to live so that he could tell the others what he saw. Killing four of them was good enough; for now anyway. That was when she decided that this is how she would kill Korean soldiers. She remembered her father telling her and Ann about how he and Wu terrorized the North Koreans this way. Now she would do it. Hit here and then run. Hit there and then run. She would use those gorilla tactics from now on.

With her teeth grinding Jenifer looked back through the trees at the North Koreans jumping out of the trucks and circling around the guns. The soldier that had passed out was awake but not making any since to the lieutenant. He had gone mad; slipping off into insanity.

"I might not have sent you to hell but what I did give you was good enough." Jenifer whispered.

Jenifer turned and left the area before the Korean soldier started checking the woods. She headed to the north a few miles and then turned to the east. She wanted to make few hits in Marquez. By time it started getting dark Jenifer found another shack. This one was in better shape. From there she could see the northern part of the town of Marquez about four hundreds yards off. But she was tired and decided to get some sleep. She would hit any Koreans she saw the next day.

When Jenifer woke up the next morning she looked towards the town of Marquez. Four Korean soldiers were standing in front of the Exxon gas station. They were laughing until one of them fell to the ground. The others were checking him when another one of them fell. The other two quickly got their rifles ready as they looked around. A third one fell and the last one got behind a stack of old tires.

Knowing that she was out of range of the soldier's AK-47 Jenifer stood in plane sight. Then she screamed like she had done so many times. The soldier dropped his rifle and started running as he screamed.

"Three down and another one ... crazy." she whispered to herself. After letting out a heavy sigh she added; "Good enough."

As the Korean solder continued to run Jenifer looked at him with half open cold eyes. Her entire family was now dead so she had no reason to care for her own safety. On the other hand she had to live so she could continue feeding her rage. She just wanted to kill Korean soldier; and maybe drive one mad every now and then.

Jenifer sat down in the shed so no one would see her. Wondering what she should do next she stood again and looked around. She saw no one; no Korean soldiers and no American citizens. Then she remembered that the citizens were to scared to come out, during the daylight hours anyway.

Realizing that she had not made any hits in or around the town of Jewett for a long time she decided to go there. There was a nice barracks there full of Korean soldiers just waiting to get shot and she was more than happy to help them with that. Just as she started to step out of the shed she heard something.

A black drone flew within feet of Jenifer's face. It should have checked out the shed but for some reason it did not. The drone continued to fly towards the Exxon station in Marquez. When it got to the dead Korean soldiers it hovered a few feet from them for a while. A few minutes later two more black drones flew in from the north. Then they left in different directions just as two trucks of Korean soldiers drove in.

The trucks drove into the Exxon station and stopped. The Korean soldiers piled out of the trucks and surrounded the gas station. Jenifer knew that she probably could take a shot or two but, she might be seen. She would have no chance against two squads of Korean soldiers. She knew that she had to get out of the area and quickly. Sticking close to the ground she crawled out of he shed and towards the north. A few minutes later she came to a large group of trees. From there she stood and quickly walked out of he area.

That evening Jenifer came upon a house where a young man was working in his garden. It was a small garden but he probably used all of the seeds he had. She needed food badly so she decided to see if the man would give her any help.

"Hello." Jenifer said as she walked out of the trees.

Seeing her rifle the man became scared. "Who are you?"

"My name is Jenifer." she told him. "I'm not going to hurt you. I mean you no harm."

The man took a deep breath and let it out. "You don't see many people carrying a rifle ... just the soldiers." Then he remembered hearing about a small group of resistant fighters called the Ghost Warriors. "Are you one of the ... Ghost Warriors?"

Jenifer looked down and replied. "I'm the only one left now. They killed my sister and the others the other day." Then she looked up and asked; "Do you have any food to spare?"

"For you ... of course I do." the man advised.

The man lead Jenifer into his home where he cut off a chunk of smoked bacon. "It's smoked so you can eat it like this." he said as he handed the chunk of bacon to Jenifer.

The two talked for a long time. When Jenifer finished the meat the man cut two more pieces and handed her one. He ate the other one. The man's name was Jake. His wife and son had been killed by the Korean soldier a year earlier. Jenifer offered Jake a chance to get even by joining forces with her but he declined. But he did offer her a safe house when she was in the area.

Jake was a Christian reading his Bible almost all of the time so, Jenifer did not worry for her safety. She spent the night on Jake's couch which was more comfortable than it looked. It sure beat sleeping on the cold wet ground. Jenifer slept well all night getting some well deserved rest.

The next morning Jake was up before Jenifer and had breakfast ready by time she got up. He had taken some of the smoked bacon and cut it into strips and fried it. Because hungry people kept taking his chickens he moved them into a back room of his home. Jenifer ate her fill of bacon and eggs before leaving.

Before leaving Jake said; "Wait a minute. I have something that I know you can use."

Then he left and walked to one of the back bedrooms. When he came back he was carrying something wrapped in brown paper.

"My brother was in the army and sent this to me before he was killed. He was hoping that I might ... do what you're doing. But ... I'm a coward." He looked at Jenifer and added. "You're not so ... this belongs to you."

Jenifer tore the paper open and held strips of burlap in her hands. "What is this?"

"It's a ghillie suit." he said. "It's already put together."

Jenifer opened the ghillie suit and slung it over her head sliding her head through the hole. Jake walked behind her and handed her strings on each side.

"You pull these strings up to your waste and tie them in front." Jake told her. "When you want to stalk someone and you're laying down just untie the strings and the ghillie suit will cover your feet."

"Thanks Jake." Jenifer said as she gave him a big hug. "This will come in handy."

Jake took what was left of the smoked bacon and put it in a pillow case. Then he handed it to Jenifer. "You might get hungry before you find any food."

After giving Jake another hug Jenifer walked off. Something told her to stop and talk to Jake and she was glad she did. She now had a great ghillie suit and enough smoked bacon to last her almost a week.

It took Jenifer four days to get to the outskirts of Jewett. Knowing that the best tree cover was on the western side of Jewett she headed there. It was daylight when she entered the heavy tree cover but it was dangerous to be moving during that time. She waited until it was almost dark before she continued.

Her target was the new Korean soldier barracks at the northern end of town. The problem was that the trees were so close to the barracks; right up against it. She would have to find a spot to fire from giving her at least two to three hundred yards from her target. She found that spot farther to the north.

The trees behind the barracks extended farther to the north. She could set up there and fire down the edge of the tree line to the front of the barracks. This spot also put her close to other buildings where she could be spotted by civilians. Her new ghillie suit would come in handy.

When it was almost dark Jenifer slowly moved northward through the trees until she reached the spot that she had spotted earlier. Even though she had her ghillie suit she still covered herself with dead cedar limbs. As she lay there she could see the front of the barracks about three hundred yards off. She slid her rifle out from under her right arm and extended the bipod. Then she removed the lens covers from her scope and looked through it.

Four or five North Koran soldiers stood outside in front of the barracks laughing. Jenifer took aim at one of them and pulled the trigger. He fell leaving his friends wondering what happened. Before they could look their friend over another one of them fell. The other two darted into the barracks.

Seconds later the entire barracks ran outside and hid behind what ever they could find. Not knowing where the shots were coming from many of them were still easy targets for Jenifer. One by one other Korean soldiers fell to their death. Four times she reloaded her rifle until she saw movement close in front of her. It was a Korean soldier walking towards her and he was only about ten feet away.

Jenifer pulled her rifle back under her collapsing the bipod Then she lowered her head to cover her face. She hoped that the darkness of the night would help to hide her. Then she started wondering if her feet were exposed. She could do nothing as the Korean soldier was only six feet in front of her by then.

Jenifer heard at least three Korean soldiers talking to each other. One even stepped on Jenifer's right elbow. Thinking he had stepped on a dead tree limb he continued to walk on. Then he stepped on her right foot and just stood there. Did he know he was standing on someone's foot? Was he standing on her foot just to hurt her? The soldiers moved on leaving her ankle hurting.

Jenifer did not move all night. She had not heard anyone since the Korean soldier was standing on her foot. She knew that sooner or later she had to get out of there so she took a chance and slowly rolled over. To he surprise; on her right was a Korean soldier sitting on a log facing the other direction. He had a sniper's rifle and was waiting to see the person that had killed fourteen of his friends. She slowly pulled her six inch dagger from its sheath and lunged at the soldier. Before he could react she grabbed his mouth with her left hand and slid her dagger between the soldier's ribs piercing his heart. Just to make sure she did it right she stabbed him three more times and then sliced his throat.

Before leaving Jenifer looked at the sniper's rifle. It was a longer version of the AK-47. She had seen these before and smashed the rifle against a tree. Then she took a grenade from the soldier's belt and stuffed it in her backpack. With daylight coming soon she slipped away to the north.

About five days later Jenifer found herself knocking on Jake's back door. She had left most of her ammunition hidden in one of his walls so she would not have to carry it all. Jake had set her up with a bedroom of her own where she kept her rifle and other gear. After shedding her heavy jacket she walked into the den where Jake had a fire going in the fireplace.

Jenifer sat down in one of the large padded chairs in front of the fireplace while Jake was in the kitchen cooking up some homemade venison chili. A few minutes later he walked into the den with two glasses of his moonshine. After handing one of the glasses to Jenifer he also sat down.

Jake set his glass down and handed Jenifer the latest newspaper. "You're becoming famous." he said.

"What do you mean?" Jenifer asked as she opened the paper. "I've just been walking the woods." she added with a smile.

"That paper says that you've been killing a lot of Korean soldiers." Jake advised her. "They are calling you the Ghost Warrior ... actually ... the last of the ghost Warriors."

"That's about it." she said.

Jake said nothing else for a while and gave Jenifer a chance to read the newspaper. When she finished she lay the newspaper down and looked at Jake with a big smile.

"What are you smiling about?" Jake asked.

"The only thing they told the truth about was that they killed my sister and the others." she advised. "They didn't mention all of the Korean soldiers I killed at the barracks in

Jewett or the three soldiers I killed in Marquez. According to these ... pages of lies ... I only killed a couple of their soldiers." Jenifer looked at Jake with a big smile and added; "Guess I'll just have to go back out and kill a few more."

The next morning Jenifer add more ammunition to her backpack. Jake gave her some venison jerky that he had made after her last visit. Before leaving Jenifer gave Jake another long hug.

"I'll take care of your food." Jake said. "Just kill as many of those North Korean sons of whores as you can."

"You know me." Jenifer said. "I'll do my best."

Jenifer turned and disappeared into the darkness of the woods. Jake stood there watching as if she was going to turn around and come right back. Then he went back into his home and sat in his chair in front of the fireplace. Jenifer did not know it but she held a special place in Jake's heart. Good women were hard to find and Jake was looking at Jenifer as someone to spend the rest of his life with. But he had already told her that he was a coward and did not like fighting. What good woman would want a man like that?

Late that evening she found herself almost walking out into a field. There were no trees for a long ways. She decided to wait where she was until the darkness of the night came.

Jenifer had noticed that the closest group of trees was off to the west so when it got dark enough she headed in that direction. The only targets to the west were the fuel depot west of Marquez and the warehouse construction just northeast of Franklin. She lost Myers at the warehouse construction site so she owed them visit. Actually; the Ghost Warrior owed them a visit.

Before getting to the river Jenifer crossed Highway 79 to its south side and went to where the Ghost Warriors had crossed when Myers was caught. When she got to the crossing where she would walk across large limestone rocks she saw that someone had left a rope tied to trees on both sides. She quickly used the rope and crossed the river. Once on the other side of the river she quickly got away from the area. If Korean soldiers had left the rope then she did not want them catching her. Then again; why would Korean soldiers cross there when the bridge was only half a mile upstream?

After walking about two miles from the river Jenifer turned north and found Highway 79 later in the evening. When it was dark enough she crossed the highway and continued north for about half a mile. By then it was to dark to see so she settled down under a cedar tree for the night. That night she heard at least two black drones searching the woods for campfires. This was why she could never have a campfire for cooking or to keep her warm.

The next morning Jenifer woke up to finches singing. She always loved listening to them in the early mornings. She got her things together and headed west. Before long she could hear the sounds of men talking. Slowly moving towards the sounds and staying low she took one step at a time until she reached a spot where she could see the fence around the warehouses.

Most of the men were at a line of tables eating but some had already walked over to their jobs on the warehouses. From where she was she could only see one guard tower but she knew there were others. The rising morning sun would soon have her in the light so she cut a few tree branches and covered herself. She would spend at least half of the day watching and learning. With her ghillie suit extended to cover her feet she relaxed to do some reconnaissance work.

As the sun came up Jenifer continued to watch through her scope all of the work that was being done. She wanted to move closer but something told her not to. It was a good thing that she listened to her intuition. Later on in the morning she got a visit.

Around nine in the morning a Korean patrol walked by. They stopped to rest and most of them sat and lay on the ground. If she had moved up to where she wanted then the patrol would have been sitting on top of her. With the Korean soldiers only fifteen feet in front of her she slowly slid her rifle back collapsing the bipod on itself. Then she continued to slide her rifle under her ghillie suit.

For almost thirty minutes the Korean soldiers did not move. They groaned a lot and rubbed their feet but they did not move. Finally the Sergeant stood and gave an order. The soldiers got up as quickly as they could and marched off. The soldiers did not impress Jenifer at all. They acted like they had no interest in walking patrol. Maybe they were being ordered to walk to much judging by how many of them were rubbing their feet.

Jenifer knew that it would be getting dark soon so she decided to move closer to the edge of the trees where she would be able to see more. With the patrol being gone a few minutes earlier she did not worry about them coming by again until the next day. By then she would be long gone.

Jenifer moved up closer to the edge of the trees keeping her ghillie suit covering her. She also drug a few cedar tree branches to cover her a little more. She could now see the entire warehouse construction site. Not knowing that Myers was already dead she scanned the area looking for him. Not finding him she took aim at the Korean soldier in the closest tower.

Jenifer pulled the trigger and the soldier in the tower dropped to the floor. She took aim and shot four more Korean soldiers before any of them knew that they were being shot at. A siren started blowing and everyone ran for cover. Not knowing that the shooter was friendly even the prisoners ran for cover. By time Jenifer had her fill of dead Korean soldiers she had killed twenty four of them. Thanks to the silencer on her rifle the Koreans in the construction site still did not know where the shots were coming from. With a smile on her face she crawled off to the north and left the area.

Being low on ammunition again Jenifer had no choice but to go back to Jake's home where she had more hidden in one of his walls. When she got to the river she found that the rope was gone but the river was down enough that she did not need it. By time she was across the river it was getting dark so she found a dry area among some yaupon bushes and rested for

the night.

Chapter 11

Death Ghost

After Jenifer crossed the river the rains came again. Because of this it took almost a week for her to get to Jake's home. That night she and Jake sat in the two high back chairs in front of his fireplace and talked. He handed her the newest copy of the newspaper and started giving her the run down of what all was in it. She would still read it but she liked hearing Jake's input on what he read.

"They're calling you the Death Ghost now." Jake told Jenifer as he smiled. "The Korean soldiers are scared to death ... you might say. This ... Death Ghost is shooting them and they never hear a thing."

"Yeah! I enjoy my job." Jenifer said. "Not to many people can say that anymore."

"Not to many people can say they have a job." Jake added.

Jenifer continued to read the newspaper. In another article it mentioned that three Korean soldiers had been killed in Marquez by a high powered 270 caliber rifle. Many of the murdered Korean soldiers had been killed with a 270 caliber rifle and it was believer that the female Ghost Warrior was the one behind the murders. The article went on to say that from that moment on two Americans would be executed for every Korean soldier that is shot by a 270 caliber rifle.

"Oh my." Jenifer whispered. "Now they are going to start executing Americans for every Korean soldier that I kill."

"Yeah ... I forgot to mention that." Jake said. "Sorry about that."

"What can I do now?" Jenifer asked. If I continue to kill Korean soldier and Americans are executed for it then that will turn the people against me."

Jenifer and Jake discussed the matter for almost two hours

and came up with not one solution. If Jenifer stopped her attacks against the Chinese and North Koreans then innocent American lives would be spared but, the enemy would never be chased out. The United States would never be freed. If she continued to kill Korean soldiers then the Americans would blame her on their family and friends being executed.

Jenifer left Jake in the den and went to her bedroom. After laying in bed she asked God for help.

"Father ... I am faced with yet another problem and I cannot decide what I should do. You know the pros and cons and what I should do. Please tell me what you want me to do."

Jenifer fell asleep before she could finish her prayer. That night she had a dream that she would never forget. In the dream she was fighting North Korean soldiers and her rifle never ran out of ammunition. She continued to pull the trigger as if she had no worry of reloading her rifle. But this was impossible as her 270 rifle only held four rounds at a time. She was also doing all of this during the daylight with the sun always behind her.

Jenifer woke up around 2:00 a.m. and got up. She built a fire in Jake's fireplace and sat in one of the high back chairs. As she watched the fire slowly getting bigger she slipped off to sleep again. Then she had another dream.

In this dream she was standing in a field. Thousands of Korean soldier were running towards her. Suddenly the field started burning between her and the Korean soldiers and the wind blew the fire towards the soldiers. She stood there not firing a shot and watched the fire consumed every Korean soldier at the other end of the field.

Suddenly Jenifer woke up when Jake lay his hand on her right shoulder. As Jake sat in his chair she told him about her two dreams. When she finished Jake sat there for a while saying nothing. He just stared into the fire as if he was ignoring her. Then he spoke.

"Sounds to me like God answered your prayer." Jake said.

Jenifer sat there quiet as she tried to make any since of her dreams. "If God was telling me something then he needs to get more clearer in his messages."

"You said that in your first dream you had an endless amount of ammunition in your rifle. I think God wants you to continue doing what you have been doing and his protection of you will be as endless as the ammunition in your dream." Jake cleared his throat and continued. "In your second dream the enemy was wiped out in front of you. I think God was telling you that he would take care of your enemies ..."

"Yes?" Jenifer said. "And what?"

"I think God is going to take care of your enemies ... the ones that come after you. You're not going to have to worry about them."

"How do you know all of this?" Jenifer asked.

"I don't know." Jake said. "I ... just ... seem to know."

"Make sure you live up to your name." Jake advised.

"What do you mean?"

"Well ... they call you the Death Ghost." Jake reminded her. "Go live up to your name."

Jenifer and Jake talked for a while and then she got ready to leave. Jake advised her to wait until it got dark before she left but she had such an uncontrollable urge to leave then. As soon as she left out the back door of Jake's home she headed into the woods. She had no plan and left it to God.

By time it started to get dark Jenifer had walked only four miles. She sat down against a large oak tree. Right beside the oak tree was a large cedar tree which gave her cover from any black drones that might fly over during the night. During the night she woke up many times thinking of that day when she killed so many Korean soldiers in Centerville. When she woke up seeing that the sun was about to rise she got up. After slinging on her backpack and grabbing her rifle she started to head south but something told her to head north.

Was God telling her to go back to Dallas? Did he want her to go home? The idea of going back to Centerville and killing a bunch of the North Koreans there still weighed heavily on her mind but, she still continued to head north.

A few days later she noticed a Korean convoy of vehicles heading north on Highway 39. She had accidentally traveled to close to the highway but no one saw her. She continued to fallow the highway until the next day when she came upon Highway 164. Standing about two hundred yards from the Highway 39 and highway 164 intersection she saw a company of Korean soldiers camped there.

Jenifer looked around and found the area completely flat giving her no place to set up for an attack. The grass was about four feet high so she would not even be able to fire from a kneeling position.

How am I going to live up to my name if I can't fire my rifle? Jenifer asked herself. Then she noticed a home that had been abandoned long ago on the other side of Highway 39. She would have to wait until it got dark before she could cross the highway.

The abandoned home was not all that great for a place for Jenifer to attack from but it was about four hundred yards from the Korean soldiers. It was good enough to fire from since she had the silencer. She crept up close to the highway and crossed when it was dark enough. When she got to the home she looked back to make sure that she was not being fallowed. Then she went inside.

As soon as Jenifer walked in the back door she realized that she was in the kitchen. The refrigerator, stove, and everything else had been removed by others needing the things. She walked from the kitchen into the den where she found a folding table in the corner. When she looked out the window she could see the campfire in the Korean camp. After moving the table over closer to the window she set up to fire her 270.

Jenifer walked back to the back door and looked around. With the full moon she could see the trees not far from the back of the house. They would give her cover as she escaped. She walked back to the den and looked towards the Korean camp. Their campfire lit up the entire camp so she took aim at one soldier. When she noticed another soldier out away from the others she thought that it would be best to shoot him first. She took aim and pulled the trigger. The soldier fell to the ground.

Then as she looked through her scope she noticed one of the soldiers yelling at a few of the others. He was a Chinese officer so she took aim and fired dropping him to the ground as he was yelling. This alerted the others which started hiding behind things. There were only a few vehicles to hid behind and a pile of gravel. Unfortunately; not knowing where the shot came from they hid on the same side that Jenifer was on. She shot three more of the soldiers before they realized from what direction the bullets were coming from.

Jenifer wasted no time getting out of the home. When she got to the trees she stopped and looked back. A few minutes later she could see shadows moving inside the home that she was just in. She aimed at one of the shadows and fired but was not sure if she hit anything of not. Suddenly bullets started hitting the trees around her so she left the area and headed east.

By morning Jenifer was three miles from where she had attacked the Korean soldiers. She turned south and headed back to Jake's home. Two days later she was walking in his back door.

"Back so soon?" Jake asked. "Miss me?"

"I killed a few more Korean soldiers but as I was leaving … running away something told me to come back here." Jenifer said. "Are you okay?"

"Never been better."

Jake had cooked up some squirrel soup so the two of them sat in the den and talked. Jenifer told Jake about her attack on the North Koreans and how she got back to his house. Suddenly someone kicked the back door but it did not open. Jenifer was in her room in a split second to get her rifle from the wall but who ever kicked the door was now in the home. Quickly she dove out of the bedroom window and hid in the bushes.

Jenifer watched from only feet away as Korean soldiers

walked into her bedroom and looked around. Not finding anything they went back into the kitchen.

Jenifer could hear the soldiers beating Jake and asking him who else was there. The second bowl of soup told them that someone had been there. When the soldiers left she noticed that at least one stayed behind. He set up in the woods just a few feet into the trees to the back of the home. He was a sniper hoping to catch the allusive Death Ghost.

Jenifer only had her knife which was on her side. She slowly pulled the knife and lay closer to the ground. The clouds covered the moon making it harder for the soldier to see Jenifer but she knew right where he was. The only chance she had was to cross the open grassy part of Jake's back yard and get into the trees where the sniper was. Laying as close to the ground as she could she began to cross the grass.

Jenifer was almost at the line of trees when another Korean soldier walked out of the back door and yelled at the sniper. She lay still as the two soldiers talked. Then the second soldier walked back into the home. Now she knew that there were at least two Korean soldiers there and maybe more. With the second soldier back in the home she continued to crawl into the trees.

With a large oak tree between Jenifer and the sniper she stood and looked around the tree at the sniper. He was young and not paying attention to what he was doing. Jenifer went back to the ground and crawled to within five feet of the sniper. Moving as slow as she could, crawling to the sniper took almost an hour. A few minutes later she found herself standing on the opposite side of the tree than the sniper was.

With her knife in hand Jenifer looked around the tree and saw that the sniper was looking away from her. With her left hand she grabbed the sniper's hair and pulled his head back. A quick move sliced his throat almost from ear to ear. She quickly grabbed his rifle and went into the trees.

The rifle was a longer barreled AK-47. It fired the 7.62x39 round which was a little bigger and more powerful than the .223 caliber fired by the M-16. Jenifer did not consider it a very good sniper round but the rifle itself did look impressive. It was not her 270 rifle but at least she now had a rifle. But one question bothered her. Was Jake still alive?

Jenifer checked the rifle and found it fully loaded. She had no idea as to how many Koreans there might be in the home. As she approached the back door to the home she could hear the Korean language being spoken. That meant that there had to be at least two soldiers in the home. She slowly stepped in through the open door and saw three Korean soldiers in the den. She raised her new rifle and opened fire killing all three of the Korean soldiers before they knew what was happening. Another soldier ran in the front door and Jenifer killed him before he even saw her.

Taking her time Jenifer checked the house for anymore Korean soldiers. There were none so she filled her backpack with food and as much of the 7.62 ammunition that she could carry. *So you'll kill innocent Americans the next time the 270 is used to kill your soldiers. Fine! I'll kill them with this thing.* She thought to herself as she held tight to the AK-47 sniper's rifle.

Jenifer reloaded her rifle and threw on her backpack. Jake was not there so he was probably taken as a prisoner. She knew that he would probably be taken to Centerville and there would be no saving him from there. After one more look around she headed for Centerville.

Two days later a serious winter storm came through dropping the daytime temperature below twenty degrees. The nights were below zero. It never got this cold in this part of Texas. Although Jenifer had a warm winter coat it was not a coat for this cold of weather. Each night she piled thick cedar limbs on the windward side of a tree and then sat on the other side of the tree. Still it was very cold with her not moving to stay warm. The cold front only lasted four days and by then she was only two or three days from Centerville.

On the day that Jenifer came to Centerville she found where she had fired from before. Again she covered herself with cedar limbs and lay down overlooking Interstate 45. She lay there for a long time before falling asleep.

The next morning Jenifer woke up with a tree limb poking her in the back of the neck. Suddenly a boot stepped beside her head and a hand reached down and grabbed her rifle. Instantly she whipped around on her back and tried to pull her knife. That was when she realized that it was not a tree limb that was poking her in the back of the neck. It was the business end of a rifle barrel. She had allowed a Korean patrol to capture her.

As Jenifer stood one of the soldiers walked up to her. With a big smile he turned her around and placed handcuffs on her wrist. She counted nine soldiers there. Nine of them had sneaked up on her and now she would be going to prison; if she was lucky.

The soldiers took Jenifer to a truck out on Highway 7. Two soldiers help her into the back of the truck and then got in with her. Another soldier got behind the wheel while the others walked back into town. When the truck got to the courthouse it stopped. Jenifer was taken out of the truck and then she stood there with the two soldiers with her. The driver went inside and came back out about two minutes later.

As the soldier walked back to the truck Jenifer noticed the officer standing at the door of the courthouse. She did not know him but he was staring her down. With a wave from this officer the two soldiers held onto Jenifer's arm and lead her up the steps and into the building. After walking up the stares in the building they turned to the left and walked into an office. One of the soldiers removed her handcuffs and forced her into a chair. Then the handcuffs were put back on her right wrist and the arm of the chair.

A few minutes later someone walked into the office and then around Jenifer's left side. When he sat down in his chair Jenifer noticed that it was the officer that was at the door.

"I am Captain Lee ... the commanding officer of a special unit formed for only one purpose ... to find you and your sister and end your terror."

"You're the terror you son of a whore." Jenifer said with her teeth grinding. "Aren't you the commanding officer of that Communist group of traitor Americans ... The Communist

League?"

"Actually it's the New Communist League and a lieutenant is their commanding officer and he reports to me.' Lee corrected her. "We got your sister and the others but you … somehow slipped away. But that doesn't matter. We have you now and all of the terrorist actions will now stop."

"There's more out there than just me you know." Jenifer advised the Captain.

"Maybe so but you seemed to be much more organized. It was hard to catch you." Lee said. "The New Communist League is wiping them all out as we speak."

"Each day you communist bastards are loosing ground to the Free American military." she reminded Lee.

Captain Lee got angry with Jenifer's comment. He quickly stood and walked around his desk to Jenifer. When he was close enough he slapped her with the back of his hand. Then he knocked her out with a second backhand.

Jenifer woke up laying on the floor of a cell. She looked around and found only one cot. No one else was in the cell. There were no windows so she had no idea what time it might be. She walked over to the door and looked through the bars in the door window. One Korean soldier stood outside in the hallway. He looked at her for just a second with no expression on his face and then looked straight ahead again.

Jenifer walked over to the corner of the cell and started to use the stainless steal commode but it had been used and not flushed. She tried to flush it but there was no water. Forcing herself she sat down on the commode and; did her thing.

Late that evening the door opened and a bowl of rice was set just inside the cell. Then the door closed and was relocked. Jenifer picked up the bowl and saw that there was no spoon but, the ball that they called rice was easily eaten by hand. After finishing her ball of rice she sat the empty bowl on the floor by the door. A couple of hours later someone opened the door and got the bowl. Then the door was closed and relocked.

It was cold that night. There were no blankets but at least Jenifer had a cot to keep her off of the cold cement floor. As she lay there she could hear screams every now and then. It was easy to tell that the person was not screaming out of frustration. They were being tortured. She wondered how much torture she might be able to handle.

The next morning two soldiers came into her cell and took her to the Captain's office again. Again she was handcuffed to the chair. Only then did she realize that the chair was bolted to the floor. This kept anyone from jumping up and trying to escape with the chair.

"I found out a little more about you ... Death Ghost ... or should I say Jenifer ... Blake?" the Captain said with a big smile. "I knew your father and I think your grandfather as well."

"I don't know who you're talking about." Jenifer confessed. "My grandfather and father are in north Texas and my name is Janeene."

Captain Lee just set there staring at Jenifer and smiling. "Well you don't have to worry." he assured her. "I'm not having you executed. I want to show you off for a while before I put you in prison."

The captain gave orders to the two soldiers standing behind Jenifer. They took her to another cell where nineteen others were. Once inside she was shown the last bunk; a top bunk. Seeing this as an non-defendable place to be she chose to pull the mattress off of her bunk and lay it on the floor in the corner where she could watch everyone else.

"You don't need to worry about any of us you know." a woman to Jenifer's left said. The woman was laying in the bottom bunk just three feet from her. "My name is Judith but just call me Judy."

Jenifer rolled over and stuck out her hand. "My name is Janeene." she told Judy not wanting to let any spies know who she really was.

The two women talked for a while and then the door opened to the cellblock. In stepped three soldiers who grabbed one of the women and took her out. The door slammed shut and was locked.

"You'll get used to that." Judy told Jenifer. Every night they come and get one of us to sleep with one of the officers. You either do it or you don't come back."

Jenifer knew that she had to do something quick. The last thing she needed was to get pregnant from a Chinese or North Korean. "I'll bite his ..."

Jenifer was suddenly interrupted by a scream from the hallway. The woman that was just taken out was resisting the soldiers. Again she screamed as the soldiers slapped her. Then she screamed again and then one of the soldiers yelled. Next was a sound that sent chills down the backbone of every woman there. It was a gunshot. The commotion in the hall stopped. There were a few voices and then the three soldiers came back into the cellblock. They grabbed one of the women by the door and drug her out. Knowing what the other woman got for resisting she did not resist.

Jenifer took a deep breath and let it out. She looked at Judy but neither said a thing. That night Jenifer did not sleep well. It was around three in the morning before she finally fell asleep. But at 6:00 a.m. everyone was awaken when two soldiers brought the woman back in.

Although the woman had been grabbed by the cellblock door her bunk was right above Judy. No one helped the young woman as she staggered back to her bunk. Being weak she could not climb up to her bunk so Judy allowed her to lay on her bunk.

The young woman's name was Bethany but Judy said that she went by Beth. She had been traumatized a great deal and only made a few inhuman sounds every now and then. What ever they did to her or made her do really messed her up bad. That night Judy slept in the top bunk. Again Jenifer did not get much sleep.

About an hour after falling asleep Jenifer woke up to voices. She looked over at Beth who was crying with three of the other women trying to calm her. Judy looked over at Jenifer and told her that seven of the Korean soldiers had raped her and four others forced her to perform oral sex on them.

Jenifer remembered what the captain had said about not wanting to execute her and wanting to show her off. "I'll take care of this." she told Judy.

"What are you going to do?" Judy asked.

Jenifer smiled real big and replied; "I'm gon'a kill me some soldiers."

It was not long when the cellblock door opened and three soldiers stepped in. Jenifer quickly walked towards the soldiers. They grabbed her and took her to the captain's office again. This was not what she had expected. With her right wrist handcuffed to the chair she was doing nothing.

When the captain walked in Jenifer quickly yelled; "I've got to talk to you Captain."

"Oh I need to talk to you too Miss Blake." he advised her.

"I told you … I'm not who you think I am." she said.

"Then … tell me exactly who you are."

"My name is Janeene not … Jenifer was it?"

"Okay … Janeene. That's what we will put on your headstone." the captain said.

Jenifer smiled and said; "I'm a Christian so I don't care what you put on my headstone. I will be in Heaven having the time of my … new life."

"I think you would call me an Atheist." the captain said. "I am not so stupid to believe in an all knowing god that controls our lives."

"He doesn't control our lives." Jenifer said trying not to show her anger. "He guides us."

The captain laughed and said; "Well I just cannot believe that. We guide ourselves through life. We make choices in our lives and our lives either get better or worse depending on the choices we make. And that's all that is to it."

"I still need to talk to you about something." Jenifer reminded the captain.

"And just what is that?"

Jenifer told Captain Lee about the young woman in her cellblock that was raped multiple times the previous night. She told him how that the woman was treated and how it effected the woman. "Why do you allow this?" she asked.

An angry look came over the Captain's face. "You're the enemy. We don't like you. My soldiers need women and this keeps them from raping all of the woman out there. Maybe you shouldn't be a prisoner."

Jenifer was taken back to her cellblock. She went straight back to her mattress and lay down. Then she looked over to Judy who was looking at her waiting to hear how she was.

"Oh ... I had to see Captain Lee. That's all." she said.

"So you weren't raped or forced to do anything?"

"No but I did talk to him about Beth and others being raped." she said. "He didn't seem to care. He even called it a way of keeping his soldiers from raping women all the time. Then he said that maybe we shouldn't be prisoners."

"Then there's no way to stop it." Judy said as she slumped done into her bunk.

"Actually there is." Jenifer suggested.

"What do you mean?"

We all need to decide which is worse ... doing what they want and letting them rape us or die maiming or killing a few of them before they can kill us."

Judy perked up. "What do you mean maiming them?"

"If they try to force you to give them oral sex ... test the sharpness of your teeth." she said with a smile.

"I think I would rather die but take at least one of them with me." Judy said with a big smile. "He wouldn't be raping anyone anymore."

Chapter 12

My Home

It had been a week since Jenifer was taken to Captain Lee's office. Over the past seven nights a woman was taken away to please Lee's soldiers and a few of them fallowed Jenifer's suggestion. They bit off the protruding part that men are usually so proud of. That night no soldiers came to grab a woman. The women that cooperated with the soldiers were brought back to the cellblock crying and sometimes bruised up some. Those that resisted and did some biting were never seen again.

The next morning three soldiers came into the cellblock and got Jenifer. "I guess I'm going for breakfast." she yelled back at Judy. She was almost disappointed when she was taken back to Captain Lee's office.

"I have someone that wants to meet you … Jenifer." Lee said.

At that time the door opened behind Jenifer but she was unable to look back to see who it was. A few seconds later Lieutenant Colonel Haung and Eve walked around Jenifer's left side and stood beside the Captain.

"Yap! That's her." Eve said. "She's the leader of the Ghost Warriors."

"Who's this whore?" Jenifer asked Lee.

Eve stepped beside Jenifer and slapped her. "I'm not a whore."

"Like I asked; who is this whore?" This time Eve slapped her harder.

"I don't know who you are Bitch but I am going to kill you some day." Jenifer swore.

"She said that her name was Janeene." Lee told Haung.

"But she was found with one of our sniper rifles?" Haung

asked. "She didn't have a 270 rifle?"

Lt. Colonel Haung and Captain Lee talked for a while not sure what to do with her. Finally Haung said that Jenifer was not the Death Ghost and then ordered him to send her to the warehouse construction. When Haung and Eve left Lee sat down just staring at Jenifer.

"I know who you are even if he does not." Lee said. He was disappointed and now that he would not be able to show off his great prize. After a few seconds of giving Jenifer the staring treatment he ordered the two soldiers to take her back to the cellblock.

Once Jenifer lay back down on her mattress she told Judy what all happened. Beth was sitting up now and even talking some. She also told Judy that she was being transferred to the warehouse construction site in Franklin. Around noon two soldiers came and got Jenifer again. She thought that she was being taken to Franklin then but she was not. A minute later she found herself in the medical room of the jail.

Jenifer was told that she was being given a few shots because a few diseases at the construction site. As she was given the injections she noticed that one of them looked different. Instead of the medication being injected into her arm this one was injected just under her skin leaving a tiny knot. She pretended not to notice but she figured that it was a tracking device in case she escaped the construction site.

What Jenifer did not know was that she was being set up. On the way to the construction site she would be allowed to escape and hopefully go get her 270 rifle. Haung wanted the rifle more than her.

After a fake medical exam Jenifer was taken to a transport van where she was forced in the back door. Then two soldiers got in with her and a third soldier closed the door. After waiting a few minutes a soldier got behind the wheel and drove the van away.

When the van was less than a half mile from the jail the American Air Force attacked Centerville. Most of the bombs seemed to hit down town but there was no way of knowing for sure. The driver never stopped and even picked up speed and got out of the area.

About a mile before getting to Marquez the van's motor stated spitting and sputtering. The driver pulled over. The two soldiers in the back with Jenifer also got out and allowed her to get out and stretch her legs. As the driver worked on the motor the two soldiers watched Jenifer. Jenifer noticed that trees covered both sides of Highway 7 but what could she do with two well armed soldiers watching her.

I need some help here Lord." Jenifer said quietly. *"I need to get out of here but these two soldiers aren't going to let me."*

Suddenly it got dark. Black clouds came over and blocked the sun. Rain started to fall and thunder echoed through the sky. The driver and two other soldiers quickly got into the van and shut the doors forgetting that they had a prisoner outside. With her hands cuffed she wasted no time and ran for the trees. In seconds she was out of sight.

Jenifer looked back to see the back door on the van fly open. Just to make it look good the three soldiers jumped out and looked around. Then they ran into the woods on the opposite side of the highway than Jenifer ran. Thinking that this almost looked comical she stopped and looked back again. Then she continued to run.

Not knowing that this was just a setup so that she would lead Lt. Colonel Haung to her 270 rifle she continued to run. Haung did not care about Jenifer but her rifle. The rifle of the second Mountain Ghost would be a better prize than one of the Mountain Ghost's daughters.

Jenifer was on the southern side of Highway 7 so she circled around and crossed Highway 7 farther to the east. Then she headed for Jake's home. Hopefully the Korean soldiers had not burned it down and her rifle with it. When she got back to Highway 7 she looked both ways and saw no one. After crossing she noticed a black drone hovering not more than one hundred yards away. It was watching her but not using the tiny rockets to attack her. She wondered what was going on.

While Jenifer was hiding from the drone she tried to slide her handcuffs off. She was surprised at how easily they came off. Why would the Korean soldiers put them on her so loosely? Then again, who cared. She was free and that was all that mattered.

That night Jenifer hid under a cluster of large cedar trees. She sharpened a small, green cedar limb on a rock and started picking at the tiny knot left after the shot under her skin. Before long she could see the tiny, almost invisible thing. It looked like a tiny seed. She squeezed her skin and it popped out. She could see tiny symbols on one side of the seed that looked like Korean writing. She knew then that it had to be a tracking device. She kept the tracking device hoping that she could use it later.

Jenifer was tired and weak from hunger. They were not fed much in the jail. For this reason she decided to stay where she was for at least one more day. She would set traps the next day to catch some food and build up her strength.

That night was a scary one as she kept hearing black drones flying around. She knew that they were looking for her but, should she get away from the area while it was dark? There was to much cloud covered, no moon light at all so she would not be able to see her way. However; in the daylight the black drones might find her. She decided to take her chances in the dark.

About four hours into trying to walk through the woods at night she came upon a home. No one was outside but she noticed that they had a chicken coop. She took her time and walked up to the coop and opened the door. It was easy catching a chicken as they slept.

Jenifer still had the sharpened cedar stick and poked a hole in the chicken's right thigh and slid the tracking device under it's skin. Then she let it go hoping that it might go into the woods and confuse the Chinese and North Koreans. Then she grabbed another chicken and closed the door. The chicken started cackling so she broke its neck. Then she heard movement in the home and quickly ran back into the woods.

After Jenifer was far from the home she sat down and plucked the chicken. She could not build a fire to cook the meat and had to eat it raw. Beef did not taste bad eaten raw but chicken was another story. But when you are hungry enough you would surprised at what you will eat.

With a full stomach she fell asleep. Rain woke her up all through the night as she was now wet and cold. She hoped that Jake had stored cold weather gear in the walls as well as more food. Before long she noticed that the sky was turning blue so she got ready to go again.

When Jenifer got to Jake's home she stood in the trees and watched the home for a while. Finally she moved in close to the back door which had been either blown or left open. She took a quick look inside and saw no one. Hearing nothing she moved inside the home and looked around. It looked like someone had been there but the home was empty now.

The first thing that Jenifer did was retrieve her 270 rifle. As she tore walls apart she found another backpack and filled it with 270 caliber ammunition. A few minutes later she ripped a wall apart and found canned food and pillow cases full of jerky. Suddenly she heard the sound of a vehicle's brakes squealing. Looking out the front window she saw a pickup truck. A Korean driver and two other soldiers got out. Her bolt action rifle was no match for three fully automatic AK-47s so she left out the back door.

Jenifer walked around to the side of the house with the garage. When she heard the soldiers talking in the back yard she went to their truck and got in. Wasting no time she cranked it up and took off. Just a few miles from Jake's home she passed another truck full of North Korean soldiers. She looked at her side mirror and noticed that only one of them looked at her but they did not stop or turn around to chaise her. When she came to an old driveway or road she turned in. A minute later she pulled up to a house that had been long since forgotten. Half of the roof had fallen in.

Jenifer got out of the truck and checked the house. It was

empty. She knew that she had to hide the truck before a drone found it and her. She started to get into the truck to take it someplace else when she noticed three wooden crates in the back. She drug the crates out of the pickup truck and opened them.

In the first two crates were rocket propelled grenades and in the third crate were two RPG launchers to fire them with. Jenifer drug the crates into the home and back to where the roof had caved in. She dug through the rubble and drug the crates into the hole she made. Then she covered the crates with the rubble that she had removed. No one would find the crates without taking that half of the home apart.

Jenifer went back out to the truck and drove it down the road a few miles. After driving the truck to a deep ditch she turned the motor off and got out. She did not want the truck to catch fire which would show the Korean soldiers where it was. After placing the transmission in neutral she pushed the truck into the ditch. With all of the over hanging tree limbs and brush the truck was almost completely invisible.

It was around nine the next morning before Jenifer got back to the house where she had stored the crates. Again she checked the home for anyone that might have moved in while she was gone. Then she pulled out the crate with the two RPGs in it. After removing one she pushed the crate back. Then she pulled out a crate with the rockets in it. She pulled out the vest that carried three of the rockets and put three of the rockets in it. After removing one more and putting it in the RPG launcher she slid the crate back. It still had four rockets in it.

Jenifer thought about leaving her rifle because the RPG and rockets weighed so much but, what would she do for protection? After walking around with her rifle for a while she decided to just carry the RPG and rockets. She put her rifle on top of one of the wooden crates and covered them with the rubble. She slung the vest on and attached it in front and then picked up the RPG launcher. Then she was off to the fuel depot just west of Marquez.

The next evening Jenifer was about to cross Highway 79

just north of Marquez when she saw a Korean convoy heading towards Jewett. Firing at the vehicles was so tempting that she had to bite her lips but, she held back. She wanted to hit the fuel depot a great deal more. When the convoy was long gone she crossed the highway and continued her trek to the depot.

Staying on the northern side of Highway 79 Jenifer used the dark of the night to crawl into the trees across the road from the fuel depot. She had to travel a long ways over open field to get to the trees and with an almost half moon. When she was about one hundred from the front gate of the fuel depot she settled down for the night. She was going to hit the depot in the morning but that would leave her having to cross the open fields during the day. She knew that she would never make it. She decided to wait and hit the depot the next evening so that she would have the cover of night to aid in her escape.

That night Jenifer chewed on some of the jerky that Jake had made and stored away in the walls of his home. She slept well that night although it was a bit cold. From time to time she woke up to voices but they were from the depot and not soldiers on patrol. When the sun came up she realized that she could easily be seen before long so she moved back into the trees some.

Throughout the day she spotted walking patrols but none of them came close to her. Then she realized that they did not expect someone to be so close to the depot. They were expecting someone with a high powered rifle. A few black drones flew by but that was all. By that evening it was time to move to the edge of the trees.

Jenifer knew that when she fired the first rocket the Korean soldiers would know where she was. She lay the vest beside her and got the RPG ready. If she had her rifle she would go for the guards in the towers but this was a chance to take out the large tanks. The actual tanks were underground but she hoped that the RPG rockets would hit the large pipes above ground and ignite the fuel in the tanks.

Jenifer was ready to fire as she waited for it to get dark enough to hide her for at least a couple of shots. Finally it got dark enough for her to do her thing. She took aim at the pipes to the closest tank and fired the RPG. As she quickly loaded the second rocket the first tank blew with such a large explosion that it took out the tank next to it as well. She fired the second rocket and took out the pipes to one of the middle tanks. It blew as well.

Jenifer did not know that none of the Korean soldiers were even firing at her yet. After firing the RPG a third time they knew where she was. Taking a chance on being shot she raised the RPG and fired a forth time. As she turned around she realized that the rockets had set the bushes behind her on fire. She was being profiled by the bright flames. Quickly jumping to her left she was back in the darkness of the trees and left the area.

Jenifer headed across the fields as quickly as she could. When she was about half a mile away from the depot she stopped to rest. Not meaning to she fell asleep under a small cedar tree. It got cold that night causing her to wake up a few times but she went back to sleep and slept until the morning sun came up a few hours later.

Jenifer took four days getting back to the home where she stored the weapons. She had walked right past the home and had to turn around and head back. When she got to the edge of the woods behind the home she heard voices. Then she saw three kids playing in the side yard. With her rifle hidden away in the home she was completely unarmed. Not knowing what to do she waited until it was dark. Then she would rush into the home and surprise any adults that were there.

After it was dark enough to move in Jenifer crept up to the back door. She was hoping that they were an unarmed family just wanting to survive. She listened and only heard two adults talking; a woman and a man. She slowly stepped into the back door and slowly walked into the den where the man and woman sat in front of the fireplace.

"I mean you no harm." Jenifer told the couple.

"We have no weapons." the man advised her.

"How long do you plan to be here?" she asked.

"The soldiers kicked us out of our home and then burned it down when they left." the woman said as she started crying. "There was no reason for that."

"North Koreans ..." Jenifer said. "... Trash ... every one of them."

"Your RPG is empty Ma'am." the man said with a smile. "We were planning on staying until we found a better place."

Jenifer took in a deep breath and let it out. "I have no problem with that but ... I have weapons hidden here. I need you to leave them alone."

The man pointed at Jenifer. "You're the one ... that ... Death Ghost we heard about."

"Yeah! It's me."

"We won't touch your things." the man said with big bright eyes and a big smile. "You just keep killing those Chinese and Korean bastards."

"I plan to." she assured them. "Right now I just need some rest."

With that remark Jenifer walked into the back room where the crates were and got her rifle out. Then she pilled some sheetrock up for a bed and lay down. With her rifle beside her she fell asleep.

Jenifer slept all night without waking up at all. When she got up she noticed that the family that was there the night before was gone. She was not sure if they would turn her in so she moved the rockets and extra RPG out into the woods. After piling cedar limbs over them she left looking for another hiding place for the RPG and rockets.

Jenifer was not two hundred yards from the home when she heard explosions in that direction. The man and woman must have turned her in for the reward. They might get more than they expected when the soldiers did not find her body or any weapons. She worried more for the children.

Before long she came to a place that looked familiar to her. It was the trailer that her parents lived at so many years ago. Across the field she could see the burned down home of her dad's friend Tom. She remembered the many times that her fathers sat down with her sister and her and told stories about this place. The trailer was so rotten that it was unlivable and Tom's home was burned down. But she remembered finding a home down the road in which she could hide the weapons and herself in. An hour later and just before dark she arrived at that home. No one else was there.

That night Jenifer rested in the home. She woke up all through the night worried that someone might catch her again. She knew that if she was even the guest of the Chinese or North Koreans again she would be so well guarded that escape would be impossible. When it got daylight she left to go get the RPG and rockets. One thing was for sure. She would never do anything without her father's 270 rifle being with her again.

The first time that Jenifer got to the weapons she checked out the home. It had been bombed and burned down. The Koreans wanted to make sure they destroyed the RPG and rockets. It took two full days to bring the RPG and all of the rockets back to the new hiding place. When she was finished she rested that night again.

The next morning Jenifer got up and checked the home out. In one bedroom she found clothes for a man and a woman. She considered hiding all of the weapons and staying there as the owner of the home. The best place to hide is in plane sight.

Jenifer found a wall where the nails had moved out some and pulled the nails. Then she lowered the sheetrock to the floor. By the end of the day she had a hardy hiding place for the left over RPG, rockets her 270 rifle and backpack. Then she started cleaning the home. Out the side door was a deep water well with a hand pump. After pumping the well a while she had water coming up. The first thing she did was wash the sheets and clean the bedroom. Within a week she had the home looking almost new. In the side garage she found a hammer, nails and other tools and made many repairs. She would hide in plane view as a single woman living there and make hits every now and then.

For the first week Jenifer seemed to enjoy her new home. So she might not be recognized she cut her long hair short and wore dresses she found at the home. She never wore a dress in her life. She was already looking like an American woman that was just trying to live when a North Korean patrol came by.

Jenifer was outside and saw the patrol walking up. The patrol consisted of nine Korean soldiers and three American men. The Americans wore all black so she knew them to be part of the New Communist League. One of them carried a sniper's rifle of some type. She played her part as just another American woman trying to survive.

The Sergeant walked up to Jenifer and asked who she was. She still used the name Janeene. The Sergeant asked her many questions starting with why she was there. She told him that her husband was killed by another American many months back. Then her home burned down and she left to find another place when she came upon this home.

As the Sergeant continued to talk to; Janeene, he sent four of the soldiers to search the home. A few minutes later they came back out after finding nothing. Finally the Sergeant smiled and told Jenifer that they had to move on. Then he shook her hand and the patrol left.

Jenifer had accomplished her goal in fooling the North Koreans into not seeing her as Jenifer; the Death Ghost. As far as the patrol was concerned she was just another American female trying to survive. Now she had to work on her appearance when she was the Death Ghost.

Free America was still sending jets and bombers to destroy anything that the Chinese and North Koreans had but their ground forces still had not done much. That was about to change.

One day Jenifer was working to till some ground for a small spring garden when she noticed movement in the trees behind her home.

"Come on out." Jenifer said to who ever it was thinking that it was someone that might be hungry. "I don't have much food but I can help you if your hungry."

At that time an American soldier stepped out of the trees along with many of his men. Jenifer was shocked to see the man and just stood there staring at the them.

"I'm Lieutenant Davis Ma'am." the man in front said as he stuck out his hand.

"I'm Je ..." Jenifer stopped not sure if she should give her real name. "I'm Janeene."

"Nice to meet you Ma'am." Davis said as he shook her hand. "I'm sorry if we scared you."

"Not at all." Jenifer said. "I was just surprised to see soldiers from Free America."

Jenifer invited Davis and some of his men into her home for some water. As they sat at her dinner table Davis told her many things that she did not know. Come to find out Free America now covered all states east of the Sabine River which was the eastern border with Louisiana. The only part of the old United States that the Chinese and North Koreans still held was Arizona, New Mexico and the southern half of Texas. The Chinese and North Korans had extended their control into northern Mexico and the Mexican government was even helping them. The Chinese made an agreement with the Mexican president that if Mexico helped them then they would let Mexico have Texas later. Of course this was a lie but the gullible and corrupt Mexican president actually believed them.

When Davis finished telling Jenifer what all was going on she decided to go ahead and tell him who she really was. He was shocked.

"We're actually looking for you ... as part of our mission." Davis said still shocked to find her so quickly. "But first ... can you prove that your Jenifer Blake?"

"I don't have a driver's licenses if that's what you mean." Jenifer said with a smile.

"The Jenifer we're looking for has a 270 rifle." Davis said. "I've seen it before and I'll know it if I see it again."

Jenifer got up and walked into her bedroom. Davis fallowed her. She moved a dresser and opened a door in the wall. Then she reached into the wall and pulled out her 270 rifle.

"Is this it?" Jenifer asked.

Davis looked at the silencer and smiled. "That's it. That silencer is a one of a kind made by a friend of your father's when he had the rifle."

Jenifer put the rifle backing the wall and closed the door. After moving the dresser back against the wall she and Davis walked back into the kitchen and sat back down at the table. Davis was more than pleased knowing that he had found Jenifer.

"Let me say that I'm sorry to hear about your parents." Davis said. "I really liked your dad. He loved telling stories of all that he and Wu did."

Jenifer and Davis talked for a while longer and then Davis had his men set up a camp just inside the trees. Then he sat back down and started telling Jenifer about a large ground invasion force that was being put together. He invited Jenifer to join that force but she quickly declined.

"After killing my parents I actually enjoy killing Chinese and North Koreans ... on my own terms." Jenifer assured Davis.

"We're on our way to the prison camp in Huntsville to free all of them." Davis admitted. "You want to at least join us in that?"

"That place was destroyed." Jenifer advised Davis.

"We have photographs showing that it is up and running again." Davis said. "It is so full of prisoners that we can't bomb it from the air. To many Americans would get hurt or killed."

Jenifer thought about it and agreed to go with them under one condition. No one was going to tell her not to kill as many Chinese and North Koreans as she could.

"I have no problem with that as long as you don't start shooting until I give the word." Davis said. "I don't need you rushing into things and messing up the mission."

"I can wait." Jenifer agreed. "But when I start killing those bastards just don't try telling me to stop until I feel like I'm finished."

"And I think I can agree to that." Davis assured her.

"Actually ... I was hoping that you would go. We can use a sniper with your reputation."

"And I will go as the Death Ghost." Jenifer added.

"Again ... I have no problem with that." Davis agreed again.

Chapter 13

The Mexican Connection

When Jenifer woke up the next morning she made three pots of coffee. It was all she had but she was excited about the American military being there. When Davis found out that she had used the last of her coffee for him and his men he apologized. She just smiled and said that spring was coming and there would be plenty of acorns. Oak trees produce acorns and they can be roasted and ground into coffee.

Because of the black drones and Davis had two companies of men with him they would have to move at night. Davis had no vehicles with him so he and his men walked. By the next night Jenifer, Davis and his men were on their way to the Huntsville prison.

Most of the men and women in the prison were American captives from other attacks against the Chinese and North Koreans. Jenifer did not know about any other attacks. The newspaper only told what Lieutenant Colonel Haung wanted the public to know. She was amazed at how far Free America had come into the south.

Because of them moving at night and the size of the movement it took almost two full weeks to get to the Huntsville prison. Davis made sure that they came in from the west where the trees were more abundant. Davis sent one company to the trees on the northern side of the prison. Then he got on his radio and called in the air strike. The attack on the prison and downtown Huntsville were suppose to be during the day so that the air strikes would be more accurate. Also the office buildings in Huntsville that were being used by the Chinese and North Koreans would be full of the enemy.

The old Huntsville Livestock Auction had been rebuilt into a better prison than what was there before. But it was still vulnerable to air attacks. Thirty minutes after Davis' call on his radio the jets came in and hit the guard towers of the prison. The prisoners were safe. That was Davis' cue to attack. The jets that took out the guard towers also took out parts of the fence giving Davis and his men a way into the prison.

Before moving across Interstate 45 and into the prison Davis looked at Jenifer and said; "Have fun."

Jenifer was already set up and just waiting for Davis to tell her to start firing. She smiled and looked through her riflescope and picked a target. Then she fired and took aim at another target. She continued this until she was almost out of ammunition. By time Davis and his men took over the prison Jenifer had killed fifty three Chinese and North Koreans.

Now finished she started to stand and give her blood curdling scream but she just did not have it in her. So she just stood there in her torn cloths and white skin looking like a ghost. The captured Chinese and Korean soldiers looked up and saw the ghost standing there mocking them and they were scared. Then finally she raised her rifle and screamed putting even more fear into the captured enemy soldiers.

Off to the south Jenifer could hear more explosions. American bombers had come in and were dropping bombs on office buildings in downtown Huntsville that were being used by the Chinese and North Koreans.

Jenifer just stood where she was for over an hour before slowly lowering herself to the ground where she lay down and rested. To the Chinese and Korean prisoners it looked like the ghost had melted into the ground. This started mummers among the prisoners and the legend of the Death Ghost was reborn.

That day the border between Communist held Texas and Free America moved south to cover the town of Huntsville. Within another month the line had moved south of Huntsville a few miles and formed a line almost straight east and west. Arizona was also a part of Free America.

By this time Jenifer was standing in Free America. Davis and his men had moved on to other adventures. Jenifer thought that the war for her was over but it was not. The Chinese and North Koreans left New Mexico and into Mexico where the Mexican government protected them. The only part of the old United States that the Chinese and North Koreans controlled was about one quarter of Texas; the southern quarter. The New United States was almost completely free.

Jenifer had no idea as to what was about to happen but soon she would be fighting a new enemy; the Mexican army. Helping Mexico were other countries from South and Central America all remaining under Chinese control. When spring came so did Mexico and the other countries helping them.

The Mexican president hung on to the promise that Mexico would get Texas and devoted any and all resources to take Texas. One day an entire battalion of Mexican soldiers were wiped out by American fighter jets and bombers. The Rio Grand River ran blood red for many miles. In some places of the Rio Grand River the blood was so thick that it killed many of the fish. Their floating dead bodies stank up the river so bad that no one tried crossing for along time.

American jets patrolled the Rio Grand River at all times while the military had foot soldiers pushing the line between Free America and Communist Texas farther to the south. By spring all of Texas was free but the war was not over. Although all of Texas was declared free by spring time large groups of Mexicans and soldiers from other countries were crossing over the Rio Grand River and taking over small areas only to be wiped out and pushed back across the river.

One such group of forty terrorist from Guatemala made their way into the area where Jenifer lived. Unknown to anyone else they were there specifically to destroy the VA Hospital in Waco which had hundreds of Americans in it. They were also suppose to free the Chinese and North Korean soldiers that were injured when the Huntsville prison was captured.

Davis and one company of men came through on their way to fight the Guatemalan terrorist and stopped to tell Jenifer. This time she would not be going with them. As Davis and his men left Jenifer's home she thought about this new threat. Davis had them outnumbered three to one and did not need her help but she felt compelled to do something. That was when she realized that this war might never end as long as Chinese leaders were hiding in Mexico.

The United States was the United States again but to many other countries from the south wanted it. The American military had been weakened by Liberal Communist that allowed the Chinese and North Koreans to come in before she was born. Now she felt it was her responsibility to do something.

Jenifer went into her bedroom and took off her dress and put on her camouflaged clothing. After lacing up her boots she loaded her backpack with food and ammunition. She made sure that she had also put her jar of white paste in her backpack as well. After swinging her backpack on and attaching the belt in front she grabbed her 270 rifle. Then she was off to cause as much havoc for the enemies of the new United States as she could.

Davis had already told Jenifer that there were many enemies coming out of the south to invade her newly found country and freedom. He also told her about trials that were being held in Centerville for those captured there so she heading there. She was hoping to identify a few of her favorite Chinese and North Koreans. Unknown to her most of them escaped to Mexico.

Jenifer stuck to the trees beside the highway as she always had. However; this time she only saw American soldiers and civilians. There were no North Korean soldiers out to capture or kill her. She knew that it would be easier walking on the highway so she left the trees and got on Highway 7. Before long she was standing on Highway 7 just before crossing over Interstate 45. It was something that she had never been able to do before.

Jenifer just stood there looking into the town of Centerville. It was the Trade Weekend so many, now free Americans were out trading and celebrating. After a few minutes she started walking into town. When she got to the courthouse she walked up the steps and then was stopped at the door.

No one was allowed in the courthouse while the trials were going on. Upset as she could be she sharply turned and started to leave. Then she heard a voice behind her.

"Jenifer." a man yelled. "Death Ghost." It was Lieutenant Davis.

Jenifer whipped around and walked back to the front door of the courthouse where Davis was. "I need in there." she quickly told Davis.

The lieutenant ordered the American soldier at the door to allow her in so he did. Davis and Jenifer walked up the stars to the courtroom where a major was the judge.

"I don't know why you're here." Davis asked Jenifer. "All of the Chinese and North Korean officers ran to Mexico."

Jenifer stopped on a dime. "Then who are the trials for?"

"A few North Korean sergeants and lower ranks ... that's all."

Jenifer was mad. She whipped around and started to leave. Then she remembered something.

"I thought that you and your men were chasing some terrorist or something." she asked.

"Oh they ran back across the border where half of them got shot for their troubles." Davis said with a smile. "Now half of them are forever swimming in the Rio Grand River."

Jenifer gave Davis a tight hug and then said; "Don't get to close to me. Everyman I get close to ends up dead."

"Well in that case ..." Davis said with a big smile. "... Okay!"

Jenifer turned and disappeared outside. Within minutes she was backing the woods; a habit that she just could not break. When she remembered that she was in Free America she would turn to walk the highways and roads.

That night Jenifer camped on the side of Highway 7. She even started a camp fire and cooked a rabbit that she shot. The meat tasted much better cooked. Freedom to do things like this was going to take some getting used to. Something kept telling her to camp in the woods but there were no more Chinese or North Koreans to worry about so she ate her rabbit and lay down. In seconds she was asleep. Later that night she found a reason to continue camping in the woods.

Around midnight Jenifer woke up to two men groping her. With one man holding her hands down she could not reach her rifle or knife. The other man was ripping her pants off and then her panties. Then he doubled up his fist and hit her in the face as hard as he could. She was badly dazed but not out. The man at her feet stood and unzipped his pants. By time he dropped his pants Jenifer was awake enough to do something.

Jenifer quickly raised her right foot and caught the man between the legs. With him slowly falling she kicked her right knee back and caught the other man in the face. Now both men were on the ground holding the part of their body that hurt. Jenifer jumped up with her knife in hand and slit the throat of the man that was at her feet. Then she slung her hand and sliced off the parts that he was going to use on her. Then she turned her attention to the other man.

The man was still holding his face when Jenifer sliced him across the arms. As soon as he dropped his arms she sliced his throat. With both men on the ground dead she finished the job. Already at the man that was holding his face earlier she spread his legs and savagely started slicing away. She did not stop until she had in her hands what used to be between his legs. Then she went to the other man. His pants were down so it did not take as long to take his manhood. After putting the men's body parts in their mouths she packed her gear and started to leave.

That was when she realized that she had no plans. Where was she going? What was she going to do next? She had spent all of her life preparing to fight the Chinese and North Koreans and then actually fighting them. All of the action seemed to be on the southern border with Mexico so should she head there? She had no plans and no idea what to do next so she moved deep into the trees where she knew that it would at least be safer. She would rest there that night.

What Jenifer did jot know was that in Mexico General Lee and Lieutenant Colonel Haung had a personal vendetta against Jenifer. They blamed the fall of their Communist control of the southern part of the United States on her. Instead of sending many soldiers after her they sent only five specialist in finding and killing people. These five, four men and one woman were to be the new group to find and kill Jenifer, the Death Ghost. But when their hold on southern Texas fell the five escaped to Mexico with the Chinese and North Korean officers. Now they were being sent back to find and kill the Death Ghost.

Jenifer had decided to go back to her home. She no longer had a family in Dallas so there was no reason to go back there. Once at her home she hid her 270 rifle back in the wall and carried an AK-47 she took off of a North Korean soldier after killing him.

One day Jenifer was coming back from checking a few traps that she had out when she saw heavily armed North Korean soldiers lurking around her home. She dropped the two rabbits she had and got ready for a fight. Although she knew that the war was over she also knew that the Chinese and North Koreans along with a few countries in South and Central America were still thinking that they could take Texas. This meant that the war only changed. But she did not know that anyone would send soldiers just to kill her.

Jenifer had her AK-47 with her so fighting these five should be no problem. The female Korean soldier was still outside when Jenifer walked up behind her and slit the throat. After re-sheathing her knife she just walked in the backdoor. The four men did nothing thinking that she was the woman with them. When they looked up and saw Jenifer standing there with a big smile they started to raise their rifles but they was to late. Jenifer emptied an entire thirty round magazine into the four almost cutting two of them in half.

Right at that time someone else walked in the backdoor. Jenifer swung around and pulled the trigger. She thanked God that the magazine was empty. Standing at the door was

Lieutenant Davis.

"You gon'a shoot me or just stand there and shake?" Davis asked her.

Jenifer dropped her rifle and almost jumped into his arms. She was not sure why she did that. Maybe it was the impact of killing four in a gunfight and then the shock of someone behind her and she had an empty magazine.

Davis was past his retirement. He tried to retire but the government would not allow him to do it. So he went to the armory and picked up a sniper's rifle and plenty of ammunition for it. Then he headed out to join forces with Jenifer.

The rifle that Davis chose was an older model of a M-14 using the 308 caliber ammunition. It had a 6x32 scope on it, a bipod and sling.

Davis helped Jenifer drag the bodies outside and burned them. Then they put the extra AK-47 rifles in the wall for safe keeping. After that they sat in front of the fireplace while Davis told her about many things she did not know.

One day a force of six battalions crossed the Rio Grand River into Texas. Almost eight hundred men and women, soldiers from North Korea, Mexico, Guatemala, Venezuela, and other countries in South America crossed the river in three places document Texas. They left California, Arizona, and New Mexico alone. They only wanted Texas.

One of the three groups, almost sixteen hundred soldiers that had crossed the river were headed Jenifer's way. Just the two of them fighting so many alone would be suicide.

Jenifer's fight was not over and she knew it. But from now on she would not be fighting as any ghost that stood and yelled at the enemy that she allowed to live. She and Davis would be gorilla fighters from then on. They would hit one or two targets, back off and later hit one or two targets someplace else. But for now, where should they go? Where was the enemy? Where was the fight?

Davis heard something about the six battalions crossing the river but that was all he heard. He told Jenifer but what could only two do against two of six battalions? They wanted to do something but they also wanted to live.

Jenifer knew that the enemy knew where she lived. That was how the four men and a woman knew where to find her. That meant that the Chinese and North Koreans in Mexico also knew where she lived in order to send anyone. But how did they know?

The trials in Centerville continued. When Davis and Jenifer heard that Lieutenant Fu, the mayor of Jewett was on trial they had to go see her. The thing about it was that they planned to do much more than just see her.

On the day of Fu's trial she was found guilty of many war crimes including the ordering of many American's to be executed. She was to be stood against the wall of a nearby building and shot. But Davis and Jenifer had other plans. As American soldiers walked her out of the courthouse she suddenly fell. Everyone thought that she tripped but she was dead. When she was rolled over a single bullet hole was found in her forehead. No shots were heard so the soldiers had no idea where to look for who did it. An autopsy showed that she had been shot with a 270 caliber rifle. Everyone knew that Jenifer had to have been the one that did it but it could not be proven.

A search of Jenifer's home found no 270 rifle. When asked where her rifle was she said that she lost it. Then she asked why they cared. Fu was about to be executed anyway. One of the soldiers just said that it was not the way they did things.

As the soldiers left Jenifer turned to Davis and said; "It's the way I do things."

When the American soldiers liberated the prisoner slaves at the warehouse construction site just northeast of Franklin all North Korean soldiers that were captured were placed in one of the barracks. One month after the shooting of Lieutenant Fu in Centerville the North Korean prisoners at the warehouse site were about to have their own trials.

On the morning of the trials a young man and woman dressed in American uniforms left the site after their night duty. With a few others also leaving no one thought about it except one soldier.

"I didn't know we had any female guards out here." the gate guard said to his friend.

"Neither did I but ... there she is." the friend said.

About fifteen minutes later three explosions went off completely destroying the barracks where the North Korean prisoners were being held. All of the prisoners died in the explosions or in the fire that fallowed. The only person that was suspected to have been a part of the explosions was a young, tall blond but she was not seen again.

A week later more prisoners were being transported to Centerville when the truck carrying the prisoners was stopped. A man and woman stood in the middle of the highway dressed in torn cloths and white skin. From a distance they looked like ghost but when the truck got closer the driver saw that they were human.

"Get out of the way." the driver yelled from inside the truck.

Davis walked up to the driver and ordered him and the other soldier out of the truck. Jenifer walked to the rear of the truck and ordered the soldiers out of there. Davis watched the American soldiers while Jenifer looked at the six North Korean prisoners. Then she raised her AK-47 and fired killing all of the prisoners.

Jenifer walked to the front of the truck and joined Davis. They thanked the Americans for their cooperation and then walked into the trees. Within seconds they were out of sight.

When the American soldiers were asked about the two people that killed the prisoners they could not identity them. They could only say that the man and woman wore torn clothes and a white paste covering their skin. They even had the white paste in their hair.

These hits on Chinese and North Koreans continued for over six months almost wiping out any of the enemy that remained in Texas. Only seventeen out of ninety three Chinese and North Korean prisoners ever saw prison. Davis and

Jenifer took care of the rest of them.

The American government made it a felony to cross the Rio Grand River without permission and only three spots on the border was open for crossing to the north. Anyone crossing to the north without that permission was shot on sight. No prisoners were taken.

From time to time two ghosts were seen on the Mexican border carrying high powered rifles and killing anyone in the Rio Grand River that was heading north. It did not take long for the illegal crossing into the United States to come to a complete stop.

Three months later the United States invaded Mexico. Within a week Mexico City and all land north of it was under American control. Invasions into the United States from the south stopped. For the first time in over three generations the United States was a united country again.

Seven years later a museum was built in Dallas to commemorate those that fought to free the United States. One room in that museum was dedicated just to the Blake family. Jenifer was not at the opening of the museum.

Jenifer and Davis were never seen or heard from again. At times rumors were heard about two ghost seen on the Rio Grand River at night. No longer having an enemy to fight the ghosts just walk around and no one was ever able to get close to them.

It did not matter if the rumors of these ghosts were true or not there was one thing that was true. Thanks to one family that saw it as their duty to fight the enemy, the United States was free again.

What love a man must have for his country that he chooses to lay down his life to keep that country free.

Other Publications of

Vernon Gillen

Below is a list of my other novels and books that have been published.

Novels

1. "Texas Under Siege 1."
   Tale of a Survival Group Leader.
   After a man is voted as the leader of his survival group in Texas a self proclaimed Marxist president asked the United Nations troops to come in and settle down the civil unrest. The civil unrest was really nothing but Americans that complained about how he ran the country.

2. "Texas Under Siege 2."
   The Coming Storms.
   The young group leader continues to fight when the countries that made up the United Nations troops in the United States decided to take over parts of the country for their own country's to control.

3. "Texas Under Siege 3."

The Necro Mortorses Virus.

As the group leader continues to fight the UN he learns that an old organization really controlled everything. They were known as the Bilderbergs. Tired of the resistance in Texas they release the Necro Mortorses virus also known as the zombie virus.

4. "Texas Under Siege 4."
250 Years Later.

This novel jumps 250 years into the future where the Bilderbergs are still living with modern technology while the other people have been reduced to living like the American Indians of the early 1800's. One of these young man stands up and fights the Bilderbergs with simples pears and arrows.

5. The Mountain Ghost."
Making of a Legend

The Mountain Ghost continues to fight the Chinese and North Koreans soldiers that have invaded the entire southern half of the United States.

6. "The Mountain Ghost."
The Ghost Warriors.

After Russ and June have twin girls the girls grow up and move back south to fight the Chinese and North Koreans as the Ghost Twins. Before long they grow in numbers and call themselves the Ghost Warriors.

Other Books

1. "Carnivores of Modern Day Texas."
A study of the animals in Texas that will not only kill you but in most cases will eat you.

2. "Zombies; According to Bubba"
After studying the Necro Mortises virus for my novel *Texas Under Siege 3*, I realized that I had a great deal of

information on it. After finishing the novel I wrote this book leaving the reader to make their own decision.

<u>Unpublished</u>

A great deal goes into publishing a novel or book that takes time. After I write a novel I have someone proofread it. Then I have to find an artist to draw the cover picture which is hard to do. Actually finding an artist is easy but finding one that I can afford is not so easy. Then the novel or book has to be approved by the publishing company. Only then is it published. Then you have kindle and that opens another can of worms.

The fallowing novels are unpublished as I write this but will be published soon. Keep checking Amazom.com for any new novels that I have published.

1. "The Mountain Ghost."
The Legend of Russell Blake.
After the Chinese and North Koreans attack the southern United States two young brothers, Brandon and Russell Blake go after the invading enemy. After Brandon is killed Russell smears a white past allover his exposed skin and earns the name Mountain Ghost.

2. "The Mountain Ghost."
The Ghost Soldiers.
After the death of Russell Black his son, Russ, continues as to bring death and destruction to the enemy as the new Mountain Ghost.

3. "The Glassy War."
Three thousand years in the future and three galaxies away the United Planet Counsel fight and enemy that is trying to control every galaxy they come to. After both starships crash into the planet the survivors continue to fight.

4. "The Fire Dancers."

I stopped writing this novel to start writing the Mountain Ghost series but I will be getting back to it.

I hope that you have enjoyed this novel. Please help me by sending your comments on what you thought about this novel or book by e-mailing me at bubbasbooks@msn.com . By doing this you will help me to be a better writer. You will also let me know what you, the public, is looking for in these types of novels and books. I have a very creative mind, a bit warped some say but, still creative but, I still need to know what you are looking for. I thank you for your assistance in this.

Vernon Gillen

Made in the USA
Columbia, SC
16 November 2022